ALI SPARKES
MAKERS

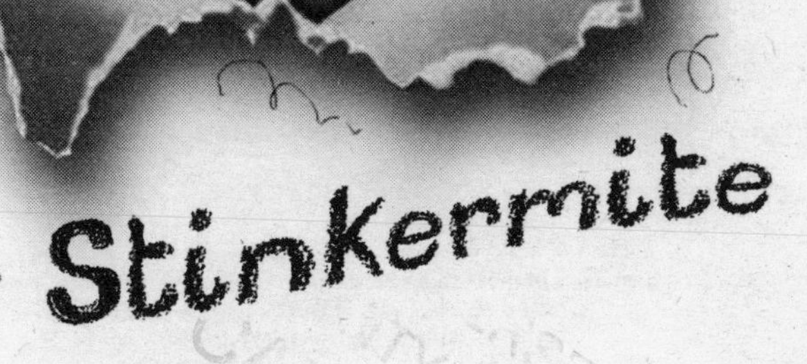
Stinkermite

To Jacob and Alex, creators of Taurs

First published in the UK in 2008 by Scholastic Children's Books
An imprint of Scholastic Ltd
Euston House, 24 Eversholt Street
London, NW1 1DB, UK
Registered office: Westfield Road, Southam, Warwickshire, CV47 0RA
SCHOLASTIC and associated logos are trademarks and or
registered trademarks of Scholastic Inc.

ISBN 978 1 407 10293 1

A CIP catalogue record for this book
is available from the British Library

Printed by
CPI Bookmarque, Croydon, CR0 4TD
Papers used by Scholastic Children's Books are made from wood grown in sustainable forests.

1 3 5 7 9 10 8 6 4 2

www.scholastic.co.uk/zone

Chapter One

Someone Get the Wire Coathangers

As the swaying head of the snake rose above his pillow, swaying, pulsating, evil, Jack screamed.

With laughter.

There was an annoyed huff from the bunk below and suddenly the snake was pulled inside out, squished up into a ball and thrown into Jack's face.

"Lewis! Get your stinky sock off my bed *now*!" bellowed Jack. "Or I'll get Krushataur to pulp your head!'

His seven-year-old brother appeared at the top of the bunk-bed ladder, retrieved the mangled cotton serpent, and threw it across the room. He looked sulky.

"You can't though, can you?" he muttered. "Because we can't make *any* of our Taurs do *anything*. It's not fair!"

"Aunt Thea will be back soon," sighed Jack. "Then we can get back to Electrotaur and Slashermite."

"*When*, soon? Everyone's been saying that for weeks and she's still not back and it's not fair."

Jack felt the same. He lay back on his pillow and wished, just as much as Lewis did, that their Aunt Thea would return. Without her they could not get to their Taurs – their very own, hand-drawn monsters – who lived underground in Tauronia, beneath the standing stone in Aunt Thea's back garden.

With Aunt Thea away they couldn't get to the garden. Or go into her cottage to get out their crayons and paper, draw the standing stone – the Gateway to Tauronia – opening and then spill magic Merrion's Mead on it, so Slashermite could come scampering up the spiral stone steps and Electrotaur could come marching up stiffly after him, his green eyes giving off sparks.

And even if they could somehow do all of this, they had promised not to. Not without Aunt Thea being there. Taurs *could* be dangerous if things got out of hand. Only last spring they'd blown up the town's power supply, set fire to a pylon and electrocuted Lewis.

"She should be back by now," Lewis was going on. "What if something's happened? What if she never comes back? What if—"

"Jack! Lewis! Come down!" Their mother's voice rang up the stairs. "You're going to have a visitor!"

"Yesss!" They beamed at each other and hurtled out of the room and downstairs. At *last*! Aunt Thea must be back from her travels! All the fun could start again.

Jack swung around the top of the stairs and slid down the banister, despite his mother's shout of disapproval. Lewis followed and a second later he and his brother stood excitedly, in their pyjamas, in the hallway.

"When? When is she coming?" asked Jack.

His mother's smile faltered . . . and now that he looked at her, he could see that it hadn't been a very convincing smile in the first place. Nor was the sweet note to her voice. "Oh – not a *she* – a *he*!" she breathed. "Fancy that!"

Nope, thought Jack, the sweet voice definitely wasn't working. It was like taking a mouthful of lemonade only to find out it was the diet kind, full of chemicals and quite revolting.

Lewis noticed Mum's smile didn't go beyond her teeth. Then he found out why.

"You'll never guess! *Timmy* is coming! To . . . to stay!" The last word came out a little shrill.

Jack and Lewis froze and then stared, horrified, at their mother, who was now picking up Scrag the cat and trying not to look them in the eye.

"Yes . . . to *stay*," she went on. "His mum and dad are having some . . . difficulties . . . and need a bit of time to themselves, so Timmy. . ." she gulped, "is coming for a visit. . ." She began to stroke Scrag's furry head vigorously, despite the cat's panicked struggles to get away. It seemed even Scrag recognized the word "Timmy".

Jack pulled his spectacles out of his pyjama jacket pocket and put them on. All of a sudden, Lewis's face sharpened up. It looked as if it had been hit with The Brick Of Horror. His teeth were almost puncturing his lower lip and one eyelid was twitching.

"How. . ." began Jack. "How . . . long?"

"Oh – I don't know," his mother was trying to

talk *through* Scrag's head now, her face buried between his ears, but they could still hear the shrill distress of her voice through the fur. "Um . . . a few days . . . I think . . . maybe, maybe. . ." Scrag growled, whacked his tail about, and spat angrily as Mum gnawed on one of his ears. ". . .longer."

"Eeeee-ooow!" Scrag clawed straight up over her face, through her hair and down her back. He was out of the house in two seconds flat. Mum patted her hair back down and coughed.

Timmy was coming.

Cousin Timmy. Nasty, thumpy, guffy Timmy, coming to stay!

"Um . . . where will he sleep?" whispered Jack,

Mum closed her eyes. "In your room," she whispered back. "Sorry . . . there's just nowhere else to put him."

"There's the shed!" whimpered Lewis. "We can . . . we can make it nice. . ."

"It'll only be for a while. While his mum and dad work things out," said Mum, clinging to the banister. "They need some space."

"Work things *out*?" spluttered Lewis. "Work things out? Well, why do they need space to do *that*? I only get half a bedroom when I need to work things out, and a bit of paper maybe. Sometimes a calculator. I don't go around making everyone leave the house for weeks on end. I mean, how complicated is this working out?"

"It's not a *sum*, you noobstick!" said Jack. "It means they're having . . . you know . . . difficulties."

"Difficulties?" squawked Lewis. "I get difficulties *every day*! That blummin' zip on my school coat is still stuck together with jam and you know what I'm like when I've eaten too much semolina. But I still don't make everyone—"

"NO! You pinhead! Difficulties with being *married*."

"Oh," said Lewis. "That sort."

Oh no . . . they might even have to be nice to their cousin now, and he was so revolting. Timmy could win an Olympic medal for breaking wind. Timmy could guff so loudly and with so much force

that it rattled window panes and took your breath away (if you hadn't had the good sense to hold it in and run from the room). If Timmy guffed in the bath it sounded like he'd just sat heavily on a duck. Wherever Timmy went to visit, at some point grown-ups would knock on the toilet door in alarm, wondering if he was torturing the dog. His bowels were so musical he had been known to attempt a performance of "One Man Went to Mow" at a party.

Rumour had it that matches and lighters of all kinds were banned in Timmy's house. Jack didn't like to picture exactly why. . .

Mum seemed to be having similar thoughts. She eyed the downstairs loo. "Remind me to get more bleach and some air-freshener," she murmured. "And a plunger. And wire coat-hangers. . ." Clearly she had not forgotten Timmy's last visit. It was the day the budgie had died.

Lewis was still twitching. He stared at the door, hanging on to Jack's arm. Then he turned to face their mother and said, in a deep, possessed-sounding voice. . .

"When?"

"Soon. . ."

"*When?*"

"Today. Better go and lock your precious stuff

away . . . I'm off to the chemist for my nerve pills. . ."

Jack wailed. "This can't be happening! This is the start of the school holidays! We should be having *fun*! Where is Aunt Thea? Where is she?"

"I don't know," said Mum, miserably. "The last I heard she was living with some Tibetan monks and making goat's cheese for the poor. I think she was planning to go to China next to learn to make fireworks. But she could be back any time . . . really. And I'm sure she"ll bring you back something exciting."

"We don't *want* anything from Tibet or China!" shouted Lewis. "We just want Aunt Thea!" And he stomped upstairs to hide his best comics.

Jack and his mum stared at each other.

"It's not a great summer for you, is it?" she sighed. "Perhaps you could camp out in the garden. . .?"

Jack winced.

"In separate tents. . .?"

Jack shook his head. "There's the wildlife to consider."

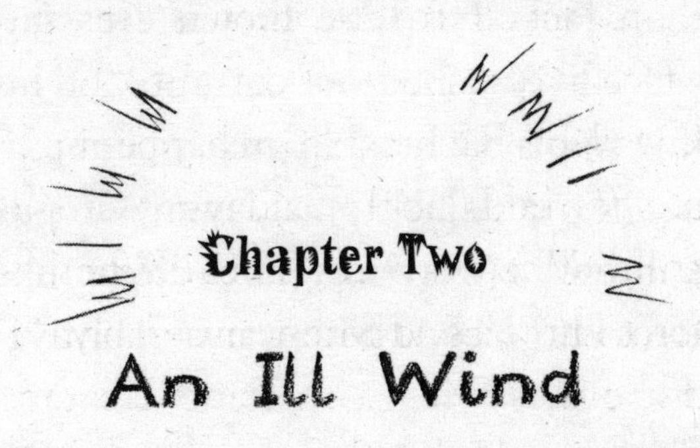

Chapter Two

An Ill Wind

Timmy arrived that afternoon. Jack answered the door and Timmy smacked him in the face.

Timmy had been bought some huge bright red comedy boxing gloves.

"Such a good idea," simpered Aunty Di, as she and Mum lugged a huge suitcase and a heavily stuffed bin bag into the hallway. "It helps Timmy get rid of his little angries."

Timmy got rid of a few more little angries on the back of Jack's neck. At ten, he was a year older and a head taller than Jack. His little brown eyes sat in his doughy face like washed-out currants and his blond hair clung to his big head in greasy clumps.

"Get *off*!" said Jack and Timmy stopped. He stood still and a worrying, soft, dream-like smile wove across his face. There was a plaintive whine from his trousers.

"Go!" shouted Lewis and the pair of them raced upstairs as fast as possible. There was a loud slam and the sound of heavy furniture being pulled up against the door.

"That's why Timmy loves it here so much!" smiled Aunty Di. "Your boys are always ready for a little game!"

Mum said nothing. She was trying very hard not to breathe in.

After half an hour in their room, Jack felt guilty about leaving Mum alone with Timmy and Aunty Di. He pulled the chest of drawers away from the door and prepared to go downstairs. Lewis remained under the bed with several action figures, fighting a bloody battle, with cries of pain and glory.

"Can't," he said, when Jack tried to get him to do the decent thing and go down too. "I'm delicate. *DIE, you DOG!*" This last remark

was directed at a baddie action figure, not his brother.

In the sitting room Timmy was grasping a jam tart in one hand and the TV control in the other, flicking through channel after channel at high speed, cranking the volume up as he went. He settled on *Who Wants to Be a Millionaire?* and started shouting answers while Mum and Aunty Di tried to talk.

"I think it's answer B, Chris," giggled the contestant. "It's a rabbit. That's my final answer."

"You dur-brain!" said Timmy.

"So how are you, love?" said Mum.

"Oh, you know. . ." said Aunty Di.

"A fish! It's a fish! You dur-brain!" bellowed Timmy.

"It'll do you and Geoffrey good to spend some more time together," said Mum.

"Yes, I think so," said Aunty Di.

"IT'S A FISH! You dur!"

"Sometimes it helps just to get a bit of a break from things."

"Hmm, well yes . . . although I'll miss—"

"DUR-BRAIN! DUR-BRAIN! FAT-FACED DUR-BRAIN!"

". . .my lovely little Timmy."

"Sausage! It's a sausage – not a country! A SAUSAGE!"

Mum winced and shot a look of despair at Jack as he stood behind the sofa.

"Timmy, love . . . can you keep it down, sweetheart. . .?" said Aunty Di. "Only Mummy and Aunty are having a little talk. . ."

"It's my favourite!" bawled Timmy through a mouthful of tart, and turned the volume up louder, while pivoting on one cheek on the leather sofa for maximum guff relief.

Aunty Di sighed and shrugged, spreading her palms. "Kids. . ." she said. "What can you do?"

"What can you?" responded Mum, kicking the plug out of the wall. The TV went *doof* and turned off. Timmy howled with shock and rage.

"Oh, sorry, love. Telly's been on the blink all week. Maybe you could run outside and play?" said Mum, smiling tightly at her nephew.

"Run outside?" Timmy looked at his aunt as if she'd just said "Run into the boiling lava pit".

"Yes, dear, you remember. That place where the air moves around and the wild creatures run away from you. . .?"

Timmy slumped back into the sofa and

rummaged in his pocket. He pulled out a PlaySquare and began to punch at it with his thumbs, emitting a volley of high-pitched beeps as he annihilated an alien attack force, and a volley of high-pitched parps as he annihilated Mum's favourite patchwork cushion.

"Come on, Timmy," sighed Jack. "Let's go outside and you can show me how good you are at PlaySquare."

Timmy shrugged and got off the sofa. Never taking his eyes off the tiny screen in his palm he shuffled out through the patio door after Jack.

"Leave the door open, please, Jack," called Mum. She smiled at him with gratitude.

Outside they sat on the edge of the decking and Timmy demonstrated his amazing skills at PlaySquare until Jack was cross-eyed, trying to follow the action on the tiny screen. He and Lewis had a PlaySquare too but they'd got bored with it fairly soon after Christmas and anyway, they had a *much* more exciting life with *real* monsters.

For Timmy though, it was thrilling, and it made him grunt with excitement. The grunts got louder and faster as the game progressed and then he'd finish up either by crowing in jubilation when he reached a new high score, or by throwing the PlaySquare down the garden when he didn't.

Jack glanced up at their bedroom window and saw Lewis watching. He made "come down!" gestures at his brother but Lewis shook his head and made throat-slitting gestures back at him. Being seven, he'd be able to claim that Jack should play with Timmy most, because Jack was nine. Jack felt his heart, already somewhere around his knees, sink into his boots.

Aunty Di stayed for tea, which they ate in the garden, even though it rained a little. "Shouldn't we go in, now?" she enquired as drops spattered against the green parasol over the garden table.

"Oooh – no! We like a little rain and fresh air, don't we, boys?" said Mum, and Jack and Lewis nodded vigorously. Mum had taken care to put Timmy downwind.

Timmy shoved a ham sandwich into his mouth without taking his eyes from the PlaySquare. There had been an attempt to get him to stop attacking Poyzoids when they had come out with the tea things, but Aunty Di had protected her son from such a wrench.

"It keeps him calm. . ." she said to Mum. "He's so sensitive, but this really keeps him calm and . . . centred." Timmy's grunts reached a crescendo and he had to be led like a blind man to his seat. Jack did manage to reach across and mute the game, so now all they had to listen to was the grunts.

"So . . . how long do you think we'll be having Timmy?" asked Mum. Jack and Lewis tensed.

"Oh . . . I don't know really . . . a little while. . ." said Aunty Di while Mum bit viciously into her sandwich and tried to smile. "Oh – I mean, I shall miss him so much. He's my little angel, aren't you, darling?"

"Duh," said Timmy.

"And I know you'll miss Mummy too, won't you, sweetheart?"

"Duh," said Timmy.

"You see . . . he's being brave but I know he's crying inside. He just holds it in. That's what he does. He holds it in."

Pweeeeaaaarreeep, went Timmy.

Aunty Di was gone by six and Mum had already set up the camp bed in their room. Lewis was horrified. The lethal end of Timmy would be at the same end as his head.

"I might never wake up again," he gulped.

Jack didn't like it much better, being up in the top bunk.

"Remember," he said, "gas rises."

It wasn't just the guffing. Jack had a friend at school with equally explosive bowels, but everyone still liked him. It was hard to like Timmy. Really hard. He had arrived in their room, flung the PlaySquare on the camp bed, and then immediately started picking up all their things and checking them over before chucking them on the floor.

"Oi!" shouted Jack. "Stop it! We just cleared up in here!" They had, too. Mum had made them do a thorough tidy of their room in readiness for Timmy's arrival.

"This is a dump," said Timmy, looking round their room. "Your computer games are pants."

"Yeah, well, we do *real* stuff. Not just *pretend* stuff on a little screen!" bit back Jack. Oh, if only Timmy knew! Where he stood right now, an eight foot, buzzing electricity monster had stood a few months back, with sparks fizzing off his hands and tail. There were still a few scorch marks on the carpet, together with the scars caused by Slashermite's finger-blades when he'd got too excited.

"You just do baby stuff like Cowboys and Indians," sneered Timmy. "Or dollies. I bet you've got dollies. Jackie want a Barbie? Jackie want a Barbie? Awwww!" Jack balled his hands into fists. "Lewis want a Teletubby!" went on Timmy, but Lewis stamped on his foot, which shut him up. He swung out a punch, but Lewis ducked easily, laughing.

"My mum says you spend all your time playing dollies with your mad Aunt Thea. She says your Aunt Thea's bonkers and shouldn't be left alone with children."

"Shut up!" snapped Jack. He knew Aunty Di didn't like Aunt Thea. They had met at some family gatherings and Aunt Thea made no secret of her disgust over Timmy's revolting habits. She

had once suggested they set him in concrete below the waist.

"Aunt Thea, Aunt Thea! She smells like diarrhoea!" chanted Timmy, seeing that he was really getting somewhere now.

Lewis grabbed Timmy's PlaySquare and held it out of the window, dangling it between finger and thumb. Jack grinned. "Say one more bad thing about Aunt Thea and Lewis drops it!" he warned. Timmy stopped jeering and his mouth pulled tight in and looked like Scrag's bottom. Lewis brought the PlaySquare in again and dropped it on the bookshelf.

"I want the top bunk," said Timmy, abruptly, to Jack. "You can sleep on the camp bed. I'm a guest and you've got to."

"Fine," said Jack. And he meant it. At least if both he and Lewis were low down they would escape the worst of the wind, and when Timmy was asleep they'd be able to whisper together and plan all the amazing things they were going to draw for Tauronia as soon as Aunt Thea got back.

Then it hit Jack, like a stone in the chest. Oh no! Even if Aunt Thea came back right now – how were they ever going to get away from Timmy? There was no way their mum would let them go to

Aunt Thea's without taking their cousin – and there was no way they'd be able to do anything with Electrotaur and Slashermite with Timmy tagging along. Their Taurs were a total secret. The only people who knew about them were him, Lewis and Aunt Thea . . . well, a couple of others *had* met the Taurs, but they'd been hypnotized not to tell.

Jack slumped on to the camp bed, which immediately flipped up and sprung into a zigzag, its metal tubing bashing him in the lip. Jack tumbled sideways and the whole thing pitched over and landed on top of him. Timmy cackled with amusement but Lewis got down on his knees and looked under the upturned camp bed.

"You all right?" he asked, blinking at Jack under the curtain of the sleeping bag.

Jack shook his head. "I was hoping to get knocked unconscious," he sighed. "Until Timmy went back home."

Chapter Three

Entertaining Timmy

Electrotaur stood, mighty and tall and glowing, before the standing stone, blue sparks showering from his fingers and the end of his tail.

"I THIRST!" he commented.

"You should have had a drink before you left Tauronia!" pointed out Jack. "That's the rule! You get a good long drink before you come up here and then we don't have to worry about you knocking out all the town's power again . . . like last time!"

Electrotaur pointed his frightening face with its metallic-looking pointy teeth at Jack and glared at him. Anyone else would have screamed and run a mile – or wet their pants – but Jack knew Electrotaur well enough to recognize a guilty look when he saw it. When he and his monster had first met, along with Lewis's smaller monster, Slashermite, Electrotaur had misbehaved and run

away from his hiding place in the woods. He'd clambered up an electricity pylon, making it explode and taking out the power for the entire town.

The local fire fighters still hadn't worked out how this had happened, despite a lengthy investigation. They'd uncovered no clues other than a half-eaten smoking doughnut.

It wasn't really Electrotaur's fault. After all, Jack had *drawn* him to live on doughnuts and drinks of electricity.

"I THIRST," said Electrotaur again, looking down at his Rupert Bear trousers forlornly. He knew how to make Jack feel guilty too. They were appallingly drawn and looked – frankly – silly. Jack kept meaning to redraw them. "GET ME BATTERIES," nagged Electrotaur.

"Look, you drank all the double As last time you came up," said Jack. "You can just turn around and go back down into Tauronia and get a drink at the lightning fountain!"

"BATTERIES," insisted his creation. "I NEED BATTERIES."

Jack buried his head under his pillow.

"BATTERIES! OI! YOU! I NEED BATTERIES," grunted Electrotaur. "OI – WAKE UP, POO HEAD! GET ME SOME BATTERIES."

Oh no. It wasn't Electrotaur at all. It was Timmy, waking him up from a dream. He groaned and sat up and the camp bed immediately tried to eat him, flipping up at both ends, like the jaws of a crab. Only his sleeping bag saved him from dreadful injury.

"We haven't got any batteries," he yawned, miserably, pushing the camp bed back down flat again.

"You must have!" said Timmy. He was sitting up in Jack's bunk, his chunky legs hanging over the edge, waving his PlaySquare agitatedly. He kicked out and let his foot "swing" into Jack's head. "You've got to get me batteries!"

"We haven't got any!" said Jack, swatting his cousin's sweaty foot away and getting up to open the window. "They're all flat. We fed them to an eight foot electricity monster."

"You dur-brain!" muttered Timmy.

"Use your lead and plug thing," burbled Lewis, from the depths of his quilt.

"Dint bring it."

"Well who's the dur-brain, then?"

"You know – I thought you might all like to go out and play in the woods today," said Mum, at the breakfast table, buttering toast and grinning brightly.

Jack shivered over his boiled egg. Not just about the prospect of going out to play with Timmy, but also because the patio doors in the dining room were wide open and a cold breeze was sweeping through. It was the only way to be able to eat without gagging, while Timmy was at the table.

"'Sfreezin in 'ere," said Timmy, pouring extra sugar on his sugar-frosted chocolate nugget honey pops. This was his most favourite cereal, which his mother had brought along yesterday. There were four huge boxes of it in the kitchen.

"Fresh air!" said Mum. "We love it in this household. Better get used to it, Timmy. Anyway – you can all take a picnic if you like; spend most of the day having games and adventures. I know you love to go off and play in the woods." She smiled encouragingly at Jack and Lewis and they looked stonily back at her.

She smiled harder.

They returned faces of granite.

She smiled so hard it looked as if she was in pain.

Jack sighed and cracked. "OK. We'll go after breakfast."

Running out of batteries at least stopped Timmy staring and grunting at the PlaySquare. He

lumped along after them as they went down the side passage, past the back garden and into the woods beyond.

"Let's go to the Holes," said Lewis. "We can show him the den."

"OK," said Jack, glad that Lewis was showing some interest in entertaining Timmy.

"If he fits inside it we can bury him."

"Lewis!"

"We'd leave the food and water with him. Should last him a day or two."

Timmy had found a stick and was hitting every tree he passed with it. "Yah! Yah!" he shouted, sending freaked-out squirrels to the topmost branches.

"You go, Tim!" said Jack. "Fight off the scary bad trees."

They did take him to the Holes. They didn't really know where else to go. The Holes, as they and other local children called it, was a very large mound of earth which had been dumped in the small wood many years ago. It was covered in rhododendron bushes but in various places there were deep holes burrowed into it, made by children back in the 1960s, their dad said, when the earth was still soft. It was a sort of rabbit warren for

kids, although none of the holes had connecting tunnels. One summer, Jack and Lewis had tried to dig some connecting tunnels but the root network of the rhododendrons was too tough to get through. Would have been a bit dangerous, too, Jack now knew. Tunnels can collapse on you and kill you. It happened to kids on beaches sometimes.

Timmy wasn't impressed when they pulled back the corrugated iron sheet which covered their den. "So what?" he said. "It's a hole. Big deal."

"It's a *den*," said Jack, propping the iron sheet up, chucking his backpack with their picnic lunch down into the den after Lewis, and then scrambling in after him. The hole was big enough for all three of them. There were little niches in the earthy walls which Jack and Lewis had made earlier that summer. Inside them were glass jars with candles. In another niche, low down and covered with a lump of stone, was a box of matches wrapped in a plastic bag, which Jack used to light the candles. "See!" he said, as the light of the little candles began to glow in the dim hole. "A den! Like a cave!"

Timmy stared at the spent match in Jack's hand, his mouth hanging open. "Gimme a go," he said, trying to snatch the box.

"You don't have a *go* at matches!" said Jack, whipping the box away. "They're not toys, you idiot. I don't even let Lewis use them. Not yet. Not until he's nine."

"Well, *I'm* ten."

"Yeah – and you're an idiot. You'd set fire to a guff or something and we'd all go home with flash burns and no eyelashes."

Timmy guffed, maliciously.

"OUTSIDE when you do that!" said Jack.

"Gonna make me?" Timmy sat down with a thud and his backside quacked. He folded his arms. "Go on – make me! Or *you* can get out."

Jack and Lewis scrambled outside fast and stood up, taking deep lungfuls of fresh air.

"That's *our* den, not yours," said Lewis. "You have to do what *we* say!"

"Oh, yeah?"

"Yeah! Get out!"

"No – I'm stayin' 'ere. This is *my* den now. You can go and find your own den."

"You get out of there in thirty seconds! Or. . ."

"I'm stayin' in 'ere for as long as I like. Try an' stop me." Jack and Lewis looked at each other, and Timmy started singing, "Aunt Thea, Aunt Thea – she smells like diarrhoea!" Jack grabbed Lewis's arm

to stop him running in to punch their cousin. He put his finger to his lips and shook his head. "Aunt Thea, Aunt Thea . . . people scream whenever they see 'er," added Timmy. He sang that one a few times and then fell silent when he got no reaction.

"Lewis," whispered Jack, loudly. "Let's pretend we've gone – and as soon as he comes out we can run in and barricade him out!"

Lewis realized what his big brother was doing and grinned. "OK – let's hide," he whispered back, equally loudly. "We'll get him as soon as he comes out! I bet he won't last five minutes!"

"No, I bet he won't!" whispered back Jack, very loudly, trying hard not to laugh.

They crept away, still whispering at the tops of their voices. They didn't hide nearby at all, of course. They just kept going. When they'd left their cousin way behind, crouching smugly in his hole, they finally let out peals of laughter and then ran through the trees, whooping and giggling. Their plan to make him stay put had worked. They were Timmy-free!

"What if he does set off the candles with a build-up of guff gas?" gurgled Lewis. "Listen out for the ka-boom!"

They slowed down to a walk and made their way to the far side of the wood.

"We'll probably get into trouble," warned Jack. "We'll have to go back for him in an hour or so. He might wander off and get lost or something."

"Jack," said Lewis. "We will *always* be able to find Timmy. All we need is a pair of nostrils."

They came to the river, which was running high and fast after heavy rain earlier that week, and began to wander along the bank. The sun glinted through the trees overhead and a smell of warm greenery and earthy water made them feel much better.

"What are we going to do with him after this, though?" said Jack. "He's a nightmare. Mum wouldn't make us look after him on our own every day, would she?"

"We'll have to bargain," said Lewis. "Negotiate."

Lewis was a very good negotiator. He was great at sounding calm and reasonable when Jack would have been shouting with indignance or slamming doors. He was also very good at "The Look". Many kids tried The Look, but few could master it. Most stuck their lower lips out a little too far, or opened their eyes so wide they looked insane. Lewis always got it perfectly right – big, mournful blue eyes looking up under his light brown fringe, a slight sensitive puckering of the mouth, a gentle, wistful sigh. Nobody could outdo Lewis at The Look. It was his ultimate weapon.

Jack grinned. He knew The Look was their best hope with Mum. Then he gave a shout. "Lew!" He pointed across the river to a row of pretty stone cottages. In front of one stood a shiny black VW Beetle.

"She's back! She's back! Aunt Thea is back!"

Chapter Four

Squelches and Squibs

It was all they could do not to dive into the river and swim across. Lewis squeaked with excitement and stepped towards the water, but Jack grabbed him. "No – too deep! Too fast!"

Further upstream the river was shallower. They decided to wade across. Two minutes later they stood, soaked from the knees down, trainers squelching on Aunt Thea's front step. Jack knocked on the door. Three seconds later it flew open.

"Jack! Lewis! I was just coming to see you!" Aunt Thea beamed at them both and gave them a hug. She was wearing a long, lime-green dress with a high collar, and jewelled sandals on her feet. She looked rather exotic, with her dark red hair pulled up into a high ponytail which swung down, curling, to her shoulders.

"Well, you might as well come in, now that

you're here – oh – you might want to take off your trainers first!"

Aunt Thea poured glasses of lemonade and set a package between them on the dining table. It was a large square box, wrapped loosely in green tissue paper. The boys beamed and set to, pulling the tissue paper away with gusto. They revealed a tin, shiny and black with silver symbols all over it.

"It's Chinese writing!" said Jack.

"Yes, Jack. I bought this in Beijing." Aunt Thea smiled. "Of course, it's highly unsuitable. . ."

Jack and Lewis eased the lid off the tin and found it tightly packed with all sorts of little paper parcels, differently shaped and decorated with more of the Chinese writing.

"What are they?" said Lewis, pulling out a circular package with bright orange lettering.

"Fireworks. Original, ancient Chinese fireworks! Terribly dangerous, of course."

"And you're giving them to us?" gasped Jack.

"Well, yes – but I wouldn't expect you to set them off without me!" she laughed. "We'll have our own fireworks night. Electrotaur can set them off with a spark from his finger, and we can all stand well clear. I don't think Electrotaur and Slashermite have ever seen a firework

display – it'll be a treat for them, don't you think?"

"We can set them off around the Tauronian Stone!" said Lewis.

"I thought so, too," said Aunt Thea. "And we'll have home-made chocolate fudge and mugs of tea. I missed you both terribly while I was in China, and made up my mind that we'd celebrate getting the Taur Team back together again as soon as possible after I got back. What do you say? Tomorrow night? Just you two, me and Electrotaur and Slashermite."

Jack and Lewis whooped and jumped up and down and then they both stopped, remembering, and sank gloomily on to the sofa.

"Whatever's the matter with you both?" asked Aunt Thea.

"Timmy," they said.

"Oh," said Aunt Thea, dropping a firework back in the tin. "That's not good. How much Timmy?"

"Days and days of Timmy," whimpered Jack, dropping his face into his hands. "We're stuck with him! We can't get away from him! He's staying with us and we're supposed to look after him all the time."

"How very depressing," said Aunt Thea. "So . . . if you've got to look after him all the time, um . . . where is he now?"

"Ah," said Jack.

"Hmmm," added Lewis.

"Boys! What have you done with him?"

"Nothing," said Jack. "We just left him in a hole. In the woods. He can get out, all right. He's not trapped or anything. He nicked our den and guffed in it and then wouldn't come out, so we just, kind of . . . left him there."

Aunt Thea folded her arms and raised one eyebrow. "Jack – go and fetch him now."

"But if he comes here we can't get Electrotaur and Slashermite out!" wailed Lewis. "And we've been waiting ages and ages and ages!"

"Well, you'll just have to wait a little bit longer," said Aunt Thea, crisply. "Go on Jack, bring him back. We'll take a look and see what can be done with him. Lewis!" she snapped her fingers. "Don't try The Look! You know your big-eye mind tricks don't work on me!"

Jack went back to The Holes with a heavy heart. He didn't get as far as their den before he heard Timmy bawling through the trees. "OI! OI, you DUR-Brains! OI! Get back 'ere! I'll tell your mum! I'll get you in trouble! OI! OI!" Jack sighed and stepped out around a clump of holly bushes.

"Got bored with your den, then, did you?"

Timmy spun round. There was chocolate on his chin and the picnic bag hung limply from his shoulders. It looked like he'd eaten their lunch already. A trail of wrappers and plastic bottles and apple cores lead away behind him, back towards the den. Jack gritted his teeth. "Come on. Help me pick this lot up."

Timmy just stared at him and then said, "Pick it up yourself, four eyes."

"You know," said Jack "You could be quite nice if you were in a coma."

When he'd got all the rubbish picked up and stuffed into the backpack, which Timmy threw

down at him, he led his cousin back through the woods.

"Where we going now?" grunted Timmy.

"Aunt Thea's house," said Jack.

"Oh." Timmy didn't sound pleased. Aunt Thea was one of the few adults he knew who took absolutely no nonsense from him. Jack was sure he was quite scared of her.

"Timmy. Hello. Let's be clear," said Aunt Thea, standing on the door step. "If you break wind in my house, I'll break your legs in my garden. Do we understand each other?" Timmy looked at his soaked feet and nodded his head. Timmy burbled and Aunt Thea drew her breath in, "I believe the words you are searching for are 'Yes, Aunty, we do.'"

"Yes Aunty, we do," repeated Timmy.

"Good. Well then, come in and have some lemonade."

They found Lewis drawing at the dining table. He shot Timmy a dark look and then carried on with his drawing, which seemed to be something green and blue with bits of brown fur. With or without the Merrion's Mead, Lewis loved to draw. Jack thought it was a very good thing that Aunt Thea kept the mead at her house. Lewis did come up with some revoltingly gruesome pictures sometimes, when he was in a bloodthirsty mood. If he'd had magic mead to use as he wished, the whole country would probably be a smoking wasteland by now.

They had made rules earlier that year, when they had created Tauronia, the underground world of Taurs, for Electrotaur and Slashermite to live in. They could draw pretty much anything they wanted as long as it lived in Tauronia and didn't escape up into the real world. They would draw all kinds of weird and wonderful beasts and landscapes; rivers and seas and volcanoes and mountains – Tauronia rolled on and on, getting bigger and more fantastic with every drawing. They knew this because Slashermite would give

them a report on what was down there, every time he came up to play. "Thank you for the ant-porridge lake!" he'd say. Or, "Do you think it was a good idea to let Grippakillataur go berry-picking in the Mountainside Meadow of Madness? He ate gagaberries until he turned pink and then started crushing boulders and singing all the songs from *The Sound of Music*. It kept us awake for days!"

All kinds of things could happen down in Tauronia but they could never, ever go down there themselves. Jack and Lewis had both talked about it. When they drew the door open, in the back of the standing stone, and the light shone up and their friends began to walk up the spiral stone steps and into view, they both *longed* to run down to meet them and take a peek at the world they had created – to find out if it looked exactly the way they'd drawn it.

But Aunt Thea absolutely forbade it. Once the drawings were made real by Merrion's Mead they were real in every other sense. The chocolate statue of Jack and Lewis in Tauronia's town square, really *was* chocolate. If you bit Jack's finger off it would taste fantastic. Slashermite's top turret room in the castle he shared with Electrotaur really did have an apple-juice geyser, which shot up into the air every fifteen minutes before disappearing back down into the apple-juice pool, so he could get a fresh drink any time he wanted. Electrotaur's lightning fountain was also quite real and would electrocute anyone silly enough to touch it. And a fall into the Molten Swamps of Badcurry actually would burn you alive, in a very spicy way, in seconds. Krushataur and his big brother Grippakillataur would pulp your head as soon as look at you – and they wouldn't be pretending.

So although they yearned to go down to Tauronia, both Jack and Lewis kept their promise. And anyway, they weren't greedy. Having a Taur each to come up and play in Aunt Thea's secluded back garden was quite enough!

"So, Timmy. How are you?" asked Aunt Thea, placing his lemonade on the table in front of him.

Timmy grabbed the glass and gulped down its entire contents in five seconds before responding. A belch gurgled up his throat and he prepared to launch it noisily across the room but then caught sight of Aunt Thea's face and swallowed it back down again, with some difficulty. "Duh . . . All right," he said.

"Timmy, has nobody ever tried to teach you some basic manners?" Aunt Thea's voice was

concerned, kind even. Timmy looked confused. "Well, it's never too late to start. Perhaps, next time somebody asks you how you are, you could say 'I'm quite well thank you. How are you?' So much nicer than 'Duh'. "

Timmy looked even more confused. "Duh?" he said.

Jack wandered away into the garden. Lewis could block out Timmy quite well while he was drawing and thinking up one of his mad Taurs or Mites, but Jack found his cousin just too irritating. He walked towards the standing stone and the sun fell on to his skin and the birds chirruped and life – just half a garden away from Timmy – was so much better. The standing stone, or the Taur Stone as they often called it, was a roughly hewn column of red serpentine, standing several feet higher than Jack, shaped like a slightly crooked finger. It looked as if it might be beckoning something down out of the sky. Jack walked around it and ran his hands across the surface of the rock, which was black with myriads of little red veins and lines and splodges across it. At the back Jack felt for the little button of rock which stood out, for them to press and bring the door open. He couldn't find it. He wasn't meant to. To guard against anyone else opening the doorway to Tauronia by accident it only ever appeared after they'd drawn it on again for a new visit from their Taurs. Jack sighed and rested his forehead against the stone. How long before they could let their friends out again?

Then he noticed something leaning against the base of the stone. He stared at it and then pulled his glasses out of his pocket, put them on – and stared again.

"It *can't* be," he murmured, crouching down to look at the thing properly. But it was. Jack really *was* staring at what he thought he was staring at.

It was half a human leg.

Chapter Five

Some Body Out there

Jack took off his glasses, wiped them on his T-shirt, and then put them back on again. He *must* be mistaken. But he wasn't. It really was half a leg. A left leg. Quite a good half a left leg, if truth be told – a firm knee clad in silky golden material, a bit like the trousers people sometimes wore to go out riding, and a muscular calf disappearing into a highly polished brown leather boot, with a bit of a heel and a pointed toe. It was a man's half a leg, that much Jack

could tell, and the bit where it stopped, just above the knee, wasn't all gooey or gory or oozing blood . . . it just sort of . . . faded away.

As Jack stared and stared, he noticed that the foot was tapping its toes, somewhere inside the smart leather boot, in a jaunty rhythm. The half a leg seemed to be cheerfully hanging around, perhaps waiting to meet a friend. The one in the matching right boot, perhaps? Jack knelt down, his mouth falling open in wonder, and put a finger out to poke its shin – to see if it was *really* there.

His finger met a solid enough bit of leather and the leg suddenly turned, the toe of the boot pointing sharply at him, as if to say, "Oh! Hello there!" Then it lost its balance and fell over sideways. For a second or two it just lay there, looking a bit embarrassed. Then the foot wiggled and propelled the calf and knee along the grass towards Jack, who scrambled away from it, shaking his head in amazement, his heart thumping. He stood up, wondering what to do. He glanced at the house – he really had to show this to Lewis and Aunt Thea. The half a leg was still wriggling towards him, like a lonely puppy. Jack felt suddenly quite sorry for it. He picked it up. It weighed quite a bit and went a bit stiff and shocked in his arms at first, then

seemed to settle down. Jack walked down the garden with the half a leg in his arms and then stopped.

How on earth could he take a half a leg in to show Aunt Thea and Lewis when Timmy was there? Timmy had no idea that their lives weren't normal. As he thought this, the leg suddenly hopped out of his arms and into the flower bed.

"Hey! Wait!" said Jack, but as he watched, the leg took two more ungainly hops and then vanished into thin air.

Jack sat down on the grass and gaped at the flower bed. If it weren't for the little bit of mud that the boot had left on his T-shirt, he would have thought he had imagined the whole thing.

"Jack, dear – are you quite all right?" Aunt Thea stepped out into the garden. "You look as if you've just seen Grippakillataur in a bikini!"

"Um . . . um . . . yeah. No . . . yes, I'm fine. Just getting some air," mumbled Jack, dragging his bemused stare away from the flower bed. He would have to tell her later, when Timmy wasn't in earshot.

Back inside, Lewis was still drawing and Aunt Thea had also given Timmy some paper and crayons. He had picked up a sharpened black one

and was stabbing it through the paper again and again, creating little smudgy black holes. As he stabbed he began to tilt sideways on his chair, a familiar expression of concentration threading across his face.

"Dial 999, Jack," said Aunt Thea. "I'm about to badly injure your cousin."

Timmy froze, mid-tilt, and then got up and ran out into the garden. Jack hooted with laughter.

"What have you drawn, Lewis?" asked Aunt Thea, peering over her youngest nephew's shoulder.

"Stinkermite," giggled Lewis, holding up a picture of the green and blue thing. It had four yellow eyes, two sets of nostrils and random clumps of brown fur on its body. "He's a mite, so he's only little, but he lives on guffergy! That's guff gas energy."

"Lewis, you are revolting," said Jack, not for the first time.

Aunt Thea winced. "So, I'm guessing this is someone we know quite well," she said, pointing to the pudgy-faced blond-haired figure running away from Stinkermite. A speech bubble next to his head contained the word "Duh!" and a purple cloud was rising from his trousers, ribboning out in the direction of Stinkermite.

Lewis went on, "Stinkermite's a guff conner –

conner – you know . . . expert."

"Connoisseur," laughed Jack.

"Yeah – like wine tasters. He knows exactly what's gone into making any guff. And whose it is. He chases really smelly guffers and traps them in a giant bubble. They get all scared and let rip and then the guff vapour can build up a bit and get good and strong – then Stinkermite takes a long sniff with his prob – prob . . . that thing!" Lewis pointed to a long, pokey, straw-like nose-type thing coming out of Stinkermite's face, beneath his eyes.

"Proboscis," said Jack knowledgeably. "Like what insects have to suck up nectar."

"Yeah – proboscis! That's it," said Lewis. "But it sucks up guffergy instead! It's his quest to get the best, smelliest, most powerful guff gas energy. Stinkermite is powered by it. You mustn't ever light a match near him."

"Lewis, have I ever told you how sick you are?" asked Jack.

"He makes a zzzubbing noise like one of those mini motorbikes while it goes along. He moves really fast – and he dribbles."

"Impressively repulsive, Lewis," said Aunt Thea. "I would expect nothing less of you. And if you think any Merrion's Mead is coming within ten feet of Stinkermite, you've got another think coming!"

At this point Timmy wandered back in from the garden, looking sullen. Lewis screwed up his drawing with a grin and dropped it in the kitchen bin.

"Come along, I'll drive us all back to your house," said Aunt Thea. "I want to see your mum."

"Oh – you don't want us to stay here for a while then?" asked Jack forlornly.

"Well, of course I do," said Aunt Thea, glancing at Timmy, who had wandered into the hallway and was licking the walls, for no apparent reason. "But I have some very sensitive indoor plants and they're starting to droop."

Back at home, Timmy began to whine about batteries again, until Mum got Dad to dig some out of the emergency torch in his car. At least once he was back playing PlaySquare again, they could leave him alone in the garden. Mum let Jack make fresh sandwiches for himself and Lewis. There was

not a second of disbelief when they told her Timmy had eaten all their lunches.

"Heavens, Cara – how will you manage for more than half an hour with that odious child?" asked Aunt Thea, as Jack and Lewis munched Marmite doorsteps.

"Oh, Jack and Lewis will help out," said Mum with a brittle laugh. They both gave her another stony look. "Oh, all right, you two – I know it's not fair. I'll try to think of something for us all to do . . . You can all come out shopping with me this afternoon. We might be able to lose him in Asco's for a while."

They all sighed and looked out into the garden where Timmy was now headbutting his PlaySquare and shouting, "LET – ME – WIN!"

"So, how was Tibet . . . and China?" asked Mum, trying to ignore her nephew.

"Wonderful. I bought you some cheese," said Aunt Thea, pulling a package wrapped in white muslin out of her bag. "Made it myself. Milked the goat. . ."

Mum's smile was watery. "Lovely," she sighed.

Aunt Thea went home with a promise to see her nephews – all three of them – the following day.

"We'll have our fireworks display," she said to Jack and Lewis quietly. "We'll just have to have it without the Taurs." They drooped.

Mum packed them all in her car to do the shopping at Asco. Jack and Lewis quite often went with her and would wander off along the toys and comics aisles while she went around getting food, and then help out with bag packing at the end. It was quite a nice way to spend an hour or so, but today the Curse of Timmy settled on them like an evil fog. All the windows in the car were open, and Lewis had his head stuck outside, like a dog, nearly all the way.

"What brake horse power is this?" said Timmy, looking balefully around the interior of Mum's little yellow Ford Fiesta.

"Um . . . I don't really know," she said, pulling a face at Jack in her rear-view mirror. Timmy was in the front seat. He had demanded it as soon as they left the house, and Jack and Lewis were more than willing. Neither of them wanted to share a back seat with him.

"My dad's car's got a bigger engine than this," said Timmy. "It's a three litre and it's got turbo boost. I bet this hasn't got turbo boost, has it?"

"Um . . . no," said Mum.

"Anti-lock brakes? Side-impact airbags? Satnav? Nah . . . you haven't got any of them, have you?"

"It's got a great radio," said Mum, flicking Radio One on and turning up the volume louder than Jack and Lewis had ever heard it. Timmy's criticisms were drowned out, even though his mouth kept moving. Jack, Lewis and Mum all sang along, at the tops of their voices, to the song on the radio. Mum's eyes looked a little wild in the rear-view mirror and she was developing a twitch worse than Lewis's. It was less than twenty-four hours since Timmy had arrived.

Back in her kitchen, Aunt Thea leaned back against the sink and stared at the high cupboard. On its top shelf there were five twiggy wooden bottles containing Merrion's Mead. Aunt Thea looked at the piece of paper in her hand and shook her head.

"Really, Aramathea!" she said to herself. "This is just silly, and you know it."

She folded the paper in half and dropped it into the bin, on top of Lewis's picture of the thing with four or five eyes. Aunt Thea paused and smiled as she saw it. She picked it out of the bin, smoothed it out and looked at the picture of Stinkermite.

She dropped it back with a chuckle and then picked out her own piece of paper again and tilted her head on one side as she studied it.

"I don't know, though," she said to herself. "It might just be worth one more try. . ." She opened the cupboard and reached up. "Maybe I just need to use a bit more," she murmured, as she took the little cork out of the twiggy wooden bottle with a gentle "tuk" and poured a small river of golden-coloured liquid across the paper. It ran quickly along the crease she'd made and a little dripped off the end, into the bin. She blew on the paper, her breath pushing the mead around it, and then laid it out flat.

"Well," she said. "You never know!" A minute later, a green shadow passed by her window. Aunt Thea stood up and blinked in shock. Then her eyes dropped, guiltily, into the bin. "Oh no! Oh no, no, no. . ." she gasped. "What *have* I done?"

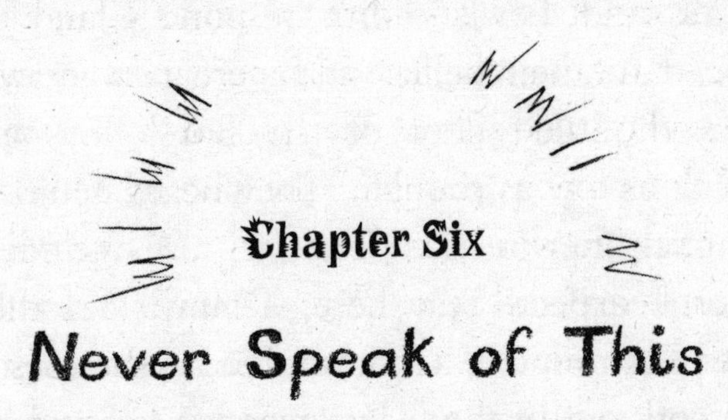

Chapter Six

Never Speak of This

"Oi! Is this one of yours?" A security guard, wearing a pale grey uniform and a peaked cap, was hauling Timmy along by his collar. Timmy was looking scared and his mouth was a vibrant shade of pink. Mum shuddered and nodded wearily. "Well, your son has just eaten all the free gifts off the front of the *Beenie* comics! You'll have to pay for them, I'm afraid."

Mum sighed. "He's not my son." But she let the security guard tip fifteen pre-school children's comics into her trolley. She hauled her nephew around to the next aisle, where Jack and Lewis instantly ducked behind the Lego display.

"Right, Timmy – you stay with Jack and Lewis and you do *not* touch *anything* – is that clear? Or I'll phone your dad. Jack? Lewis? Timmy is joining you now."

Jack and Lewis didn't respond. They had dropped to their bellies and were now crawling across the tiled floor of the Boys' Toys aisle, keeping as low as possible. They heard Mum sigh and click her teeth. "They're just round the corner, I expect. Stay here, Timmy, and they'll come back round in a minute. Look – there's some Lego you can look at." Timmy grunted and they heard his squishy expensive trainers squelching towards them.

"Quick!" gasped Lewis and he and Jack crawled swiftly round the corner before their cousin saw them. They blundered on for several feet before they realized where they were.

The horror.

Oh.

The horror.

Jack tried to stand, but his knees gave way. Lewis stayed crouched to the floor, whimpering quietly and shaking his head. "No . . . no, it can't be. . ."

The aisle stretched terrifyingly around them – an endless avenue of all that was pink and purple and fluffy and sparkly and giggly and girly.

They had stumbled into Girls' Toys!

"I never thought it would come to this," moaned

Jack, staring, powerless to resist, at a rack of My Tiny Horseys. He noted that several had glittery hooves . . . and three had a brush and comb set for their gleaming silky hair. They came with a free gold-effect charm bracelet.

Two little girls stood a few feet away, holding bead-braiding kits and staring at them. Then they giggled and turned and ran. Other girls, further away, turned to watch, like distant gazelles on a plain. One was halfway through trying on a long

pink dress from the Princess Flowerdew range, gaping at the male invaders between puffed sleeves. Princess Flowerdew herself was pirouetting on a plinth. A full-sized replica of the popular doll, her plastic hand was poised in mid-air, clutching a twinkly wand, and her plastic body was resplendent in a pink satin gown. A wispy veil and tiara thing was on her head.

"*Help . . . me. . .*" squeaked Lewis, and Jack turned to see his brother being drawn, inexorably, with small whimpers of horror, towards a huge Barbie doll's house with a shimmering pink roof and a sweeping purple staircase.

"*I can't . . . stop. . .*" Now his trembling hands were reaching for a Mermaid Barbie, which was sitting on a pink shell-shaped sofa in the doll's house sitting room. "*Just go . . . run . . . save yourself. . .*"

"The Blaine! Get the Blaine!" hissed Jack. It was all he could say to help, and at the last second, Lewis's outstretched fingers twitched and picked up Barbie's surfer boyfriend doll instead. "See – he's a bit like Action Man, isn't he? Eh? Eh?" comforted Jack, trying to avoid looking at the BabyRealLife dolls which really cried tears and really ate real baby food and really . . . oh no . . . was there no way to escape dangerous bottoms?

Even plastic ones? It was all so wrong. . .

"Like Action Man?" Lewis dropped the boy doll, the spell broken. "He's wearing a flowery shirt and a medallion! Action Man would punch his lights out."

Jack seized the moment to grab Lewis's arm and drag him back the way they'd come. Even Timmy had to be better than this. They staggered back round to the Lego display and collapsed behind it. Lewis sat up and composed himself. He clutched Jack's shoulder. "What happened back there. . ." he breathed. "We never speak of it again."

Timmy looked over the top of the display. "You two are such *girls*," he jeered. "Always playing your little make-believe games. Oooh – I live in a castle! I'm a fairy prince who fights dragons!"

Jack and Lewis stood up, defeated. They moved back into the Boys' Toys aisle, glowering.

"Anyway, you gotta stay with me, your mum says," went on Timmy. "And I wanna go and look at the bikes, so you gotta come. Or you'll be in trouble."

"Bikes? You?" said Jack. "But you hate exercise. You wouldn't *push* a bike up the *hallway* unless there was a pudding at the end of it."

"Not a stupid girly pedal bike, you dur! A motorbike."

Jack and Lewis looked at each other and then back at their cousin, who was clearly stupider than they'd given him credit for.

"Timmy," said Lewis. "Try to understand. We're in Asco's. It's a supermarket. They don't sell motorbikes."

"Well, dur! I know they don't sell proper bikes! Little ones, I mean. Kids' ones, like you see up the park. Listen – you can here 'em."

Jack and Lewis did listen. A tinny zzzubbing sound was, indeed, echoing around the supermarket. It was a vast store and they supposed that maybe Timmy was right, and around the kids' bikes and garden toys section they might well have brought in those mini scooters or motorbikes with the little buzzy engines.

"Someone's ridin' it round," said Timmy. "This way." He turned down the end of the aisle into the toilet-roll section and something flashed fast around the corner at the far end. "See!" said Timmy, and ran up the aisle towards it. Then he slipped and landed with a whump on his well-cushioned backside. There was a thin trail of pale pink watery stuff on the floor.

"You all right?" asked Jack. Timmy scrambled to his feet and carried on up the aisle. "Someone's dropped something on the floor," went on Jack, to Lewis. "Eeeuugh! They've dribbled it all along here, look. Lewis. Lewis?"

Lewis was standing quite still and looking quite pale. His eyes seemed suddenly huge in his face. "Zzzubbing," he said. "Dribbling," he added. He gulped.

"What?" said Jack, feeling very uneasy.

The zzzubbing sound suddenly got louder.

"It's comin' back this way," yelled Timmy, suddenly scooting across their path, in from another aisle. "We can stop it, push the kid off, and I can have a go!" He jumped up and down and let off several loud parps in his excitement.

"Oh no," wailed Lewis. "This can't be happening."

Skidding around the end of the toilet-roll aisle there was a zzzubbing, churning cloud of spinning green and blue and brown stuff. Bobbing along on top of it were four googly yellow eyes. From one corner of a wide grinning mouth, a steady stream of dribble hung like a pale pink cord.

Stinkermite was alive.

Chapter Seven

Misuse of a Princess

Jack managed to slap his hand across Timmy's open mouth before the scream came out. It didn't stop the scream, but it did muffle it a bit. The same couldn't be said for the other end of Timmy. Panic rendered his backside highly eloquent. The scream that didn't quite make it out from his mouth would have been drowned out in any case.

Stinkermite's eyeballs all shot out on stalks and the furry brown bits on his strange blue-green body spun around faster and faster. He looked a bit like a small, excitable car wash. He was sniffing loudly and all four eyeballs were pointing directly at Timmy.

"I thought you didn't mead him! You said you didn't!" squawked Jack in alarm, dragging Timmy backwards away from the delighted monster, which was now dribbling from *both* sides of its mouth.

"I didn't!" protested Lewis. "I screwed him up and threw him in the bin! You know Aunt Thea didn't get any mead out. I don't know how this has happened!"

"Well, it *has* happened! We've got a Taur in the real world! This is exactly what Aunt Thea is always warning us about. What are we going to do? He's going for Timmy . . . and there is – ugh – no way Timmy's going to stop producing guffs for him to chase!"

Stinkermite, with a gurgly cry of joy, was now zzzubbing fast down the aisle towards them. His legs and arms were also greeny-blue and had little clumpy hoof-like blue claws. The drool at the side of his mouth had begun to form a bubble, which was getting bigger and bigger.

"Lewis! You've got to master him! Now!" Jack looked around, eyes wild with fear – at any moment a shopper could turn the corner and see a real live Taur and there would be complete and utter panic. Nobody was ready for this!

Lewis stepped in front of his brother and cousin and held out his hand. "Stop! I command you!" he said in his most masterful voice. Stinkermite's eyeballs twisted on their stalks and looked at Lewis. The monster slowed down a bit. "Stop!"

said Lewis, again. Close up, Stinkermite wasn't that big. Thank goodness he was a Mite and smaller than the full Taurs, thought Lewis. He was probably about the same size as Jack. "You shouldn't be here!" hissed Lewis. "What are you doing out of Tauronia? Eh? Eh?"

"Questy! Questy!" giggled Stinkermite. "Must chase guff. Big guff here. Must chase."

"Oh, great," said Jack. "It's another quest fixation. *Why* do we keep giving them quests? It always ends in disaster!"

"This is not the guff you seek," said Lewis, trying to keep eye contact with Stinkermite, which wasn't at all easy when he had only two and Stinkermite had four. "This is not. . ." he said again, trying to sound mesmerizing, "the guff you seek."

"Yeah it is," giggled Stinkermite and then just zzzubbed right past him.

"No respect!" huffed Lewis, throwing himself on the floor and grabbing one of the creature's little legs. Stinkermite fell over with a squeak and then began to wriggle to get away, but Lewis grabbed his other leg too and now he dragged him sideways behind an abandoned trolley, thanking his lucky stars that he hadn't drawn the Mite to be

strong. In fact, Stinkermite, when you got hold of him, was quite weedy.

"Questy! Questy!" he whined. "Must chase guff! Big guff! High quality. Crafted from twenty per cent protein, thirty-three per cent carbohydrate, forty-eight per cent saturated fat. Eleven per cent plasticine and ninety-eight per cent sugar syrup."

"Look, I didn't say he could add up!" said Lewis as Jack's eyebrows went up. Timmy was now leaning against the moist wipes – hyperventilating.

"What are we going to do with him now?" said Jack, amazed that their luck had held this far. "We've got to get him out of here! Now! What are we going to do?!"

"I HELP," came a voice from behind him. Jack turned around and felt his eyes stretch so wide open he feared they might ping out on stalks like Stinkermite's. Standing right there, in the middle of the toilet-tissue aisle of Asco's, was Electrotaur.

Eight foot high and vibrating with electricity, sparks in his green eyes, Jack's Taur was holding something unspeakable in his clawed left hand.

"Hurry! Hurry! Take it!" came another voice and Jack whimpered with disbelief. Slashermite was here too, jiggling up and down in agitation, his finger-blades sliding in and out and clearly

itching to make short work of the quilted Andrex.

Jack decided this was all a dream again. In which case he might just as well go along with it. He took the unspeakable thing from Electrotaur's claws and held it out to Lewis.

Lewis, still holding tight to Stinkermite's struggling ankles, and getting gobs of pink dribble raining on him for his trouble, stared at the shimmering offering. It was a pink satin gown, trimmed with lace and cross-stitched with little pink jewels across the bodice.

"It's Princess Flowerdew's dress," murmured Lewis.

"No, it's not," said Jack. "It's the Dream Fairy range. You can tell by the pink jewel detail, the silver piping and the scalloped lace trim."

"No – Princess Flowerdew!" argued Lewis. "Dream Fairy is in gold and yellow, with a pleated bodice and little hearts on the sleeves and—"

"DRESS THE MITE!" cut in Electrotaur. "BE SWIFT! GUARDS COME. GUARDS COME FAST!"

Slashermite scampered to the end of the aisle and poked his purple rhino-horned head around it fearfully, nodding and wringing his hands with metallic scraping noises.

Jack and Lewis wrestled Stinkermite into the

Princess Flowerdew outfit. Stinkermite zzzubbed and gurgled and made a great deal of dribbly fuss but at last they got him covered. Lewis slapped the lacy veil and tiara thing over his wildly gyrating eyeballs just in the nick of time, as the security guard and the store manager turned the corner into the aisle. Amazingly, Electrotaur and Slashermite were now nowhere to be seen.

"Oh yes. Better get this sorted out right away," said the store manager grimly. Jack and Lewis, and even Stinkermite, froze. This was it. They were done for. "This is a staff announcement," said the store manager into his walkie-talkie thing, and his voice echoed all around the supermarket. "Can we please have a cleaner to aisle fifteen? A cleaner to aisle fifteen. Thank you." There was a click and then the store manager and security guard walked on past them, plonking a little yellow "floor wet" sign over the worst of the pink dribble as they passed.

"Having little sister troubles?" chuckled the security guard as he went by.

"Yeah!" Jack grinned and made a "what can you do?" kind of face, wondering what on earth had happened to Electrotaur and Slashermite. "She's in a tantrum because Mum won't get her any sweets!" Stinkermite kicked out an angry

greeny-blue leg, and gurgled again, but the men had walked on now and didn't see it.

"You!" said Lewis, grabbing the creature's arm now and yanking him up. "You should not be here! You shouldn't ever be outside Tauronia! Do you understand?"

"Must chase g—"

"No! Not here! You've got it wrong!"

From beneath the veil, a long green proboscis emerged, quivering pathetically.

"Oh no you don't!" said Lewis.

"Want guff," sulked Stinkermite.

"Well, you're not having any!" snapped Lewis. "And that's final!"

Jack stood, ignoring Timmy, who was still collapsed against the moist wipes in shock, and looked around for their Tauronian friends. A second later Electrotaur's head appeared, floating high beside the recycled-paper section. Jack blinked. He still couldn't be sure he wasn't dreaming. Then Slashermite's head appeared three feet below Electrotaur's.

"It's quite all right, brother of my Creator," he grinned, showing off little pointed white teeth. "The Lady Thea sent us on a quest to rescue you."

"But . . . how. . .?" Jack's mouth opened and shut like a startled fish.

"The Lady Thea created Invisitaur to shield us!"

"She did *what*?"

"Invisitaur – a Taur to shield all other Taurs from sight in times of danger! He is all around us now, like a cloak. But we must hurry. He will not last. We must take Stinkermite and go now."

"Be my guest!" said Lewis, propelling the wriggling green Princess Flowerdew-alike towards Slashermite's head. Slashermite reached out two purple hands, blades tucked in, and yanked Stinkermite towards him. Stinkermite disappeared. Electrotaur's head also disappeared.

"Couldn't you have just Invisitaured him,

rather than make us dress him up like a princess?" queried Lewis, scratching his head.

Slashermite considered this. "Umm, no," he concluded.

Jack looked at Lewis, who shrugged.

"The Lady Thea says you must bring Timmy soon," went on Slashermite. "We must hypnotize him to forget."

"Can't you just do him now?" asked Lewis, wrinkling his nose at Timmy, whose head looked even more like a pudding when it was in shock.

"Too risky," whispered Slashermite. "Not enough time before Invisitaur breaks up . . . You must also draw Stinkermite back into Tauronia. See you later, oh Creator. . ."

Then his head popped out of view too. There were a few more zzzubs and a little gurgle of annoyance, some stomps from Electrotaur and scratchy toe noises from Slashermite . . . and then, as far as they could tell, everything was back to normal.

From two aisles along, a little girl could be heard screaming, "Mummy! Mummy! Princess Flowerdew's got no clothes on!"

Chapter Eight

Midnight Beasts

"What on earth's the matter with Timmy?" asked Mum, pushing her well-laden trolley around the end of the aisle a few seconds later.

"Oh – well – he's having a bit of a turn," said Jack.

Mum sighed. "I'm not a bit surprised. He's eaten fifteen strawberry Toxos off the front of all the *Beenie* comics. He's spaced out on E-numbers, I expect."

Jack and Lewis nodded. It was a very good explanation, and they hadn't even had to think it up.

"He said he was seeing monsters," improvised Lewis. "Green bubbly monsters. We were just coming to get you. I think he was sort of dreaming."

Mum touched Timmy's forehead and his eyes clicked into focus. "Duh?" he said, and they all relaxed. Timmy was back.

He was quiet in the car on the return trip. Jack shoved him into the back seat, while Lewis went in front. Timmy stared at Jack once or twice, frowning and biting his lip. He seemed to be trying to work out what he had just seen in the toilet-tissue aisle of Asco's.

"Did that—?" he began.

"No," said Jack.

"Was I—?"

"Definitely not."

"What the—?"

"Who can say?"

"Was it?"

"All a dream? Yes."

By the time they got home, Timmy seemed to have shrugged the whole thing off and when Mum suggested he went upstairs to lie down for a while, he did just that.

"Very odd," said Mum. "I've never seen him so quiet or obedient. It's like he's been sedated. I wonder if there are any more of those *Beenie* comics for sale anywhere. . .? I think I'll phone up Woolworths and WHSmith's. We might be able to get enough strawberry Toxos to see us through a week. . ."

"Can we go over to see Aunt Thea?" asked Jack. "She wants us to. Maybe just me and Lewis this time."

But Mum shook her head. "No – it's not fair on Aunt Thea. She only got back yesterday. She needs a bit of a rest from you two."

Jack and Lewis grimaced at each other. They had to get back to the cottage and draw everything back into its proper place – *and* find out how on earth Stinkermite had come to life.

"And what about Invisitaur?" asked Jack, when he and Lewis had got out into the back garden. "Aunt Thea made a Taur! She's never done *that* before."

"We really *have* to get over there," agreed Lewis.

But they couldn't. Aunt Thea phoned a few minutes later, inviting all three boys to tea, but Mum insisted that she was being too kind and she should just have a break – and anyway, she'd already got dinner on for them all. Jack and Lewis, hanging around under the kitchen window, listening in, were biting their knuckles with frustration.

"We've *got* to get Timmy there, too," remembered Jack. "Slashermite has to hypnotize him to forget."

"Maybe he's forgotten already," said Lewis. And later, at tea, it seemed that this was right and they wouldn't have to worry.

Timmy was back to his obnoxious self, elbowing Lewis in the face so he could get to the potatoes first and belching or guffing loudly whenever he got the urge.

"Timmy, please!" said Mum, at one point, eyeing him with disgust.

"Wasn't me." He shrugged and shoved a sausage into his mouth, sideways.

As much as Jack and Lewis loathed him, they were relieved to see him behaving normally again.

After dinner they all had to sit around playing Scrabble. Timmy stole the little tiles when nobody was looking, and put down eighteen letter words in

one go. Nobody bothered to argue with him. Every time he got annoyed he would lean sideways slightly, with a look of smug concentration, and let out a feeble whine. The feeble ones smelled worse than the loud ones.

In bed that night, as soon as Timmy had started snoring up in the top bunk, Lewis leaned across to Jack on his camp bed. "Come on," he said, "I'm not waiting any longer. We've got to get over to Aunt Thea's. We can't leave her alone with Stinkermite all night!"

"Maybe she's drawn him back into Tauronia herself," whispered Jack.

"No – remember a Taur can only be directed by its own creator," hissed Lewis, sitting up and pulling on his socks.

"Well, you directed Electrotaur that time when Garsnipe tried to bulldoze the standing stone!" pointed out Jack, also grabbing his socks now. "You got him to come out of the stone, didn't you? And he's *my* creation."

"Yesss – but that was before we had made up the rules!" argued Lewis, pulling a jumper on over his pyjamas. "Don't you remember?"

He was right. As Jack and Lewis had created more and more bits of Tauronia, they'd made up lots of rules. Some of them were sensible rules,

suggested by Aunt Thea, like not ever going down there and never working with Merrion's Mead on their own, just in case.

But they'd also had a fight once, when Lewis had drawn fishnet stockings on one of Jack's Taurs and then Jack had made one of Lewis's wear frilly pants and then it all got a bit out of hand and there were headless Taurs and legless Mites scattered all over the place, in embarrassing states of dress. Electrotaur and Slashermite, on their next visit, had put in a formal complaint and then Jack and Lewis, embarrassed and feeling guilty, had made up the law that only a Taur's creator had the power to make any changes to it or to make it do things. This had stopped any more carnage or dodgy underwear situations.

Once they'd got their trainers on, Jack and Lewis grabbed their torches from under the bunk bed, and crept out of the room as Timmy slept on. They went downstairs, listening hard for any sign of their parents waking, but it was after midnight and Mum and Dad were fast asleep. Outside the house they ran quickly up the side passage and made their way across into the woods. There was a full moon and they could see quite well as they went, but once inside the wood they had to switch on their torches.

"Wow – the last time we did this was when Electrotaur and Slashermite very first came to life," remembered Jack. "We were so scared!"

"I wasn't," said Lewis.

"You *were*!"

It took them twenty minutes to pick their way through the dark woods, stumbling over low branches and listening to the tawny owls hooting through the trees.

"It's strange, isn't it?" whispered Jack. "You hear completely different noises in the woods at night. I mean – what was *that*?"

"What?" said Lewis.

"Listen – there it goes again."

Kuwhup.

"Some strange night bird, maybe," said Lewis. "The mating call of a toad? I dunno. Come on – we're nearly at the river."

Kuwhup, went the lonely toad or the night bird or whatever it was, again.

As Jack and Lewis stumbled on, woodland wildlife abruptly fell silent behind them, several mice and voles scurried back deep into the undergrowth.

And a shadow fell across the moonlit path.

Chapter Nine

The Army Chest

They got wet feet again at the river, and at Aunt Thea's front door they took off their trainers and wrung out their socks as they waited for her to answer the doorbell.

She opened the door fully dressed and obviously still very much awake. "Oh, thank heavens!" she sighed. "And about time. Lewis, please, *please* draw Stinkermite back into Tauronia."

Stinkermite was on Aunt Thea's sofa in the kitchen. He was still wearing the Princess Flowerdew frock, although he'd taken off the veil and tiara thing. He was watching the Disney Channel on her little portable TV and dribbling with excitement.

"Hello, Stinkermite," said Lewis, and his creation's four eyes swivelled round to look at him. Above his dribbly mouth, his proboscis began to grow.

"Stinkermite! I've told you about this several times now!" scolded Aunt Thea. "Put it away!"

Stinkermite froze, mid-grow, and all four eyes looked balefully at Aunt Thea. "I will – I'll do it again!" she warned, and pulled a bottle out of her pocket. The label read: *essential oil of lavender*. "He loathes the smell of anything nice," she explained. Stinkermite's proboscis was now inverting on itself and rapidly disappearing back into his face. He was muttering something bad-temperedly.

"I'll draw him into Tauronia," said Lewis. "But not until we find out how he came to life in the first place. I didn't even put any mead on him. If

they're going to start coming to life even when we don't want them to, we're in a lot of trouble."

Aunt Thea looked very uncomfortable. "Well – er – that was my fault, Lewis. I spilled some Merrion's Mead into the bin, by mistake. I guessed that the only place Stinkermite *could* come to life would be somewhere near Timmy, as you'd drawn Stinkermite chasing him. Then I phoned your home and your father told me you were all still at the supermarket. My heart nearly stopped, I can tell you! Then I realized I had to get Electrotaur and Slashermite up to come to the rescue."

Jack and Lewis nodded. One of their *other* rules was that Aunt Thea could draw out Electrotaur or Slashermite by herself if there was ever an emergency.

"Then, of course, I had to get them to you. We could just about fit into the car, but I needed to stop them being seen, so I . . . well, I created a Taur of my own, to help."

Jack and Lewis stared at their aunt. "I didn't think you could!" said Jack.

"Well, no, nor did I. I wasn't at all sure he would work – but there you are!" Aunt Thea said, suddenly seizing a cloth and wiping the dining-room table with great vigour. "I made up Invisitaur

and his job was to cloak the others and keep them out of sight, so they could get to you and help. I waited outside in the car park, as close as I could, so we could all make a get-away as soon as they'd got Stinkermite. Did it . . . did it help? I didn't hear any emergency sirens as we drove off, so I suppose it all went off OK."

Jack and Lewis told Aunt Thea everything that had happened in Asco's.

"Oh." She smiled. "So that's why Stinkermite's got a frock on. I did wonder. He seems to have become rather attached to it. . ." They gazed across at the Mite, who was absent-mindedly playing with the lacy hem of his princess dress. "Perhaps you should draw him into his own Tauronian dress shop, Lewis."

Lewis gave his aunt a *look*.

"And Timmy? Is he quite all right?" she said.

"No – he's horrible. But he always was horrible anyway," said Jack. "And he seems to think it was all a dream."

"Even so," said Aunt Thea, anxiously wringing the cloth under the tap now. "We ought to get Slashermite to hypnotize him soon, to be on the safe side."

"Where is Slashy?" asked Lewis.

"I sent him back down to Tauronia with Electrotaur when I realized I couldn't get you to come over for tea."

Jack looked out of the kitchen window into the garden and saw the standing stone, the gateway to Tauronia, gleaming in the moonlight. "And what happened to Invisitaur?"

"Yes . . . well . . . he went too. It was only Stinkermite who had to wait for Lewis. Come on, Lewis – draw him back into Tauronia. He's too revolting to stay here much longer."

"Wish I could draw *Timmy* into Tauronia, too," muttered Lewis, picking up a crayon. "Just draw him in the town square and leave him there for Grippakillataur."

"Now, you don't really mean that," sighed Aunt Thea.

A shadow in the garden caught Jack's eye. Something moving. Probably a fox or a rabbit. "Back in a mo," he said, and stepped outside the kitchen door. His bare feet on cool grass, he wandered towards the standing stone, the hair on the back of his neck prickling slightly. There! There it was again, on the bench. As he grew closer he made out an odd shape, moving awkwardly along the wooden seat. He reached

into his pocket and got out his torch. As soon as the light clicked on his mouth fell open. He really struggled to believe his eyes. It was a chest. A robust, manly chest . . . and attached to it was a muscular, manly left arm. He had thought the disembodied leg was weird enough, but this was so peculiar he thought his brain might turn inside out.

The chest was covered in bright scarlet material with gold braiding and buttons. It looked like an old-fashioned military jacket and there was a white ruffle of material down below where the chin would have been, had there been a chin. The sleeve was of the same style and at the end of it was a ruffled white cuff and a large, elegant hand. The hand was grabbing hold of the slats and hoisting its chest along the bench. Like the leg, there were no gory bits where the chest was cut off, it all just faded away discreetly.

"This has got to be a dream," said Jack aloud, and the chest suddenly turned and sat up and the hand waved up in the air as if to say "Oh hello! I say! Good to see you!". Jack stepped back, gulping.

The arm suddenly shot out towards him, making him shriek, but a second later he realized it was just trying to be polite. It was holding out its hand to be shaken. Jack gingerly leaned across and politely shook. The hand felt quite warm and dry and normal. It had a confident grasp.

"How do you do?" Jack found himself murmuring. He was a polite boy, even when he knew the object of his enquiry had no mouth with which to respond. Or vocal chords. Mustn't be prejudiced, though. You can't judge a body for . . . well . . . only being *part* of a body. That would be, um, partist. The hand made a waggling "Ah, not so bad. . ." gesture and then slumped sideways as the chest lost its balance.

"Come on – this time I'm showing you to Aunt Thea," said Jack, and went to pick up the chest and its friendly arm. But as he reached towards it, it faded away and his hands closed on nothing.

An owl hooted. "Oh . . . kay," said Jack, aloud.

Kuwhup, went the pining toad or bird or whatever.

Jack turned around. And screamed.

Chapter Ten

A Bit of a Blow

Something worse than any monster he'd ever dreamed up stood on the lawn behind him, sniggering from one end and going *kuwhup* from the other. The improved diet at Jack and Lewis's house had obviously changed the acoustic quality of Timmy's bowels.

"You thought you were so clever, dint you, you dur-brain!" sniggered Timmy. "Creepin' away in the night, trying to leave me out of everything. But I only *pretended* to be asleep, so I could hear you whispering your little girly secrets – and I know all about you and the stuff you're doing and I'm gonna tell your mum. Unless you make it worth my while *not* to!"

Timmy had also pulled on trainers and a jumper. In the light from the kitchen window he looked sweaty and excited as well as a little scared.

"I followed you all the way through the woods and you never knew!" he gloated. "Then you didn't even shut the front door properly when you got here – so I came in too and listened to everything you were saying. I know everything, I do! And if you don't let me join in, I'm going to tell – I am! I want to draw stuff and make it real too! I want a nine-hundred brake horse power car! And a motorbike. And the biggest bit of chocolate in the world. And a PlaySquare Supreme with all the games they've ever made. And my own castle."

Jack stared at Timmy, wondering how on earth things had got so horribly messed up. "You can't use the mead for stuff like that. You can only make things to go into Tauronia," he gulped. "If you try to do stuff in this world it goes wrong. It would be a disaster."

"Oh, would it?" sneered Timmy, punctuating his sneer with another stout guff. "Well, I don't care what you say. If you don't give me a bottle of

that stuff, I'm going back to your mum and dad and I'm telling them everything and they'll take all that mead stuff off you and call the police and get Aunt Thea put away in a funny farm where she belongs! She'll get locked up – you'll see. My mum always said she was a psycho nut job and she's right."

Jack didn't know what to say. He opened his mouth to speak but nothing came out. At that moment there was a loud squelchy thud and he jolted and looked around. Stuck to the kitchen window was Stinkermite. The creature had launched itself straight at the glass in its excitement, no doubt, at smelling Timmy's distinctive perfume. All those *kuwhups* had obviously built up a bit and wandered through the house.

Jack heard Lewis cry out "Oh no!" and saw his brother and Aunt Thea staring out of the back door, aghast, at the sight of Timmy. Stinkermite gurgled with delight as he slid slimily down the window pane. "Questy! Questy! Must chase! Must chase guff. . ."

Timmy looked alarmed now – clearly recognizing his attacker at Asco. "Don't you let it near me!" he yelled, but it was hopeless. Stinkermite, skinny and spry, had already wriggled along the draining

board and through a gap between Aunt Thea and Lewis and was beside Timmy in an instant. All of a sudden the purpose of the pink slime became apparent. It stopped dripping out of Stinkermite's mouth now and began, instead, to shoot out at incredible velocity, high into the air above Timmy, where it commenced spinning wildly like a weird bubble-gum lasso.

Timmy stood rooted to the spot, his piggy eyes bulging with terror, as the whirling pink gum stuff shooting out of Stinkermite began to form into a huge bubble which engulfed the boy about five seconds later.

"Oi! Lemme-out!" whimpered Timmy, still unable to move, his voice muffled by the pink bubble, which now totally enclosed him. *Khuwup*! he added. Several times. The bubble got slightly bigger.

"Good – good – guffy!" enthused Stinkermite, his proboscis now growing rapidly.

"Stinkermite! Stop that at once!" commanded Aunt Thea, but the Mite paid no attention at all.

There were several more loud *khuwups* from Timmy as he spun around inside the bubble in a panic and then Stinkermite gave a little whoop of joy and shot his proboscis into the bubble and sniffed – loud and hard – with the power of an industrial suction pump. A second later the bubble was gone and Timmy was shrink-wrapped in pink goo. He looked as if the biggest bubble-gum bubble in the world had just deflated all over him. He gasped and the pink film across his mouth sucked inwards. Lewis leaped across to him and broke the seal with his finger. Timmy sucked the air in and coughed it back out again with a sob.

"Good guffy," burbled Stinkermite. He lay flat on his back on the grass, looking dazed and happy. His eyeballs were all slightly bloodshot.

"Lewis – I *demand* that you draw Stinkermite into Tauronia *immediately*!" said Aunt Thea. Lewis rushed inside with her, and Jack saw them grab the crumpled-up drawing Lewis had made yesterday and then get a bottle of Merrion's Mead out of the cupboard. Timmy stood, shuddering and pulling the stretchy pink goo gum off his face in the moon-light, while Stinkermite continued to burble and smile contentedly, as if he'd just finished a very good Sunday roast.

"You wait," Timmy spluttered to Jack. "I'm gonna get you all for this!"

"Shut up, you idiot!" said Jack, his heart hammering inside him. In the kitchen he saw Lewis and Aunt Thea spill the mead hurriedly on to the crumpled paper for the second time, and he stared anxiously at Stinkermite, willing him to disappear.

After a few seconds, Aunt Thea and Lewis came to the back door and joined in with the anxious staring.

"It's time you went to your new home, Stinkermite," said Lewis. "You'll like it there. Loads of great whiffs. And a dress shop, if you want one. . ." he added, with a dark look at Aunt Thea.

Stinkermite smiled at Lewis, fluttering his eyeballs, and smoothing his skirt down demurely. Then there was a small pop – and he was gone.

Everyone heaved a sigh of relief. Then there was another small pop.

And Timmy was gone.

Chapter Eleven

Trouble in Tauronia

Aunt Thea crumpled on to the back step and put her hands over her mouth.

"Lewis! How did *that* happen?" cried Jack. "Where has he gone? Where is Timmy?"

Lewis looked shocked and scared. "Um . . . I *think* . . . he's in Tauronia."

Jack scrambled past Aunt Thea into the kitchen. The picture of Stinkermite lay, damp with mead, on the edge of a biscuit tin. Above the Mite, Lewis had hastily scribbled "Gows to Tauronia rite away!" in his dodgy spelling. The mead had run across Stinkermite and then, after Lewis had chucked it down in a hurry, some of it had slewed across the page . . . and reached the drawing of Timmy.

"You've *really* done it now! You donkey!" yelled Jack. "You five-star, double-decker donkey!"

"I didn't! It wasn't my fault! It was only meant

to be Stinkermite!" Lewis looked wretched and Aunt Thea was still sitting on the back step, her head in her hands.

"Why didn't you rip the Timmy bit of the drawing off? Then nothing could have got on it. What are we going to do now?"

Aunt Thea got up. "Quick," she said. "Draw him back up again. He can come up through the standing stone like Electrotaur and Slashermite. Hurry! Hurry!"

Lewis grabbed fresh paper and quickly drew Timmy walking up the spiral stone steps that led up from Tauronia to the real world above. As soon as he'd finished they spilled mead on it and then raced up the garden. Around the back of the stone the doorway was already open, a shaft of golden light shining up from it. The three of them stood there, holding their breath, waiting.

"Where *is* he?" asked Aunt Thea, after a minute. "He should be here by now! Lewis drew him out!"

"Ah. . ." Jack sighed, understanding. "But Lewis didn't create Timmy, did he? So he can't make him do anything."

"He just made him disappear into Tauronia!" snapped their aunt.

They were silent for a while, trying to work this out. At length Jack said, "He's not a Taur . . . so I don't think we can expect any of the normal rules to work. We just don't know what's going to work and what's not. I think . . . I think I should go down there."

"No!" said Aunt Thea immediately. "It's much too dangerous. We'll wait a bit longer."

Lewis had brought the drawing pad, his crayons and some mead with him and now began scribbling again. "I'm sending Slashermite to get him and bring him back," he said. "And Jack can send Electrotaur. They'll rescue him."

"Of course!" sighed Aunt Thea, as Jack hastily scribbled Electrotaur on a quest to save their cousin. "Why didn't I think of that?"

They spilled the mead and then sat and waited. Jack and Lewis couldn't help their minds wandering into what might be happening to Timmy in Tauronia. He could be tumbling along in the hot-frog rapids or swimming through the Tauronian sea chased by Aquataurian Devil Fish which blew poison-tipped mini harpoons out of their dorsal fins. He could be beating off a swarm of metal-clad stinging Insectomites in the Candyfloss Fields of Doom, where unlucky passing Taurs were lured to

pick candyfloss off bushes only to snag the trip wires which set off the alarms inside the Insectomite hives. . .

Jack gulped and tried to think about the nicer things in Tauronia. Timmy might simply have bumped into Fluffymite and been gleefully cuddled for the past ten minutes. Or perhaps he was sitting down beneath the jam-tart tree and waiting for the jam tarts to fall, always the right side up, into his lap, while the cherryade waterfall sparkled past and flowers shaped like cups, which grew along its banks, collected a nice drink for him. There were nice bits of Tauronia too . . . and a lot of them were to do with food.

Something tickled Jack's knee. In the bright moonlight he stared and stared at it. It was hair. Not just a couple of strands of hair, but a whole head of it. Rich, golden, glossy hair with a handsome wave to it, tumbling around the top of a head and curling winningly around one well-shaped ear. The owner of this glorious head of hair was nowhere to be seen. The head it reclined on stopped abruptly at the brow at the front, and one ear at the side, resting at a jaunty angle on the grass. The ear wiggled sociably at Jack as he gaped at it. What was going on?

This time, before it could vanish, Jack grabbed the hair and the chunk of head and ear attached to it, which was, again, very neat and tidy and not at all gooey or gory. He held it up and waved it at Aunt Thea and Lewis.

"Look! This is the third time I've seen a chunk of someone in your garden! What is going on?"

Lewis shouted out with shock and then peered ghoulishly under the well-conditioned golden fringe in search of dripping chunks of brain. Aunt Thea, though, clutched her throat and looked stricken. Not scared or even very surprised, but stricken . . . with embarrassment.

"Can you hear me?" Lewis was shouting into the single ear. It wiggled politely. "It can! It can hear

me!" grinned Lewis. "I say . . . what's all this ear?"

Jack and Aunt Thea gave him a look.

"This is all a bit hairy!" went on Lewis. Then, as the hair and ear began to fade away in Jack's grasp, he added solemnly: "Ear today . . . gone tomorrow. . ."

"All right. I did it," sighed Aunt Thea. "I created that luxurious head of hair."

Jack gasped. "Why?"

"Because you're worth it?" asked Lewis.

Aunt Thea gazed down into the golden light of the steps to Tauronia. "Now is really not the time to talk about it. We need to find poor Timmy. I think I'm going to have to go down there."

"No!" shouted Jack and Lewis, together.

There was a scratching noise and then they all whooped with relief as Slashermite's little purple horn turned the corner of the steps below them, followed by the rest of his purple head and body. But Slashermite looked anxious and he was alone.

"Oh, Creator!" he cried, as soon as he saw Lewis. "Oh, what is to be done? Your cousin will not come with us! He will not leave!"

"What?" said Jack. "But he must be terrified!"

"No, he is not. He is in the Tauronian town square, drinking from the lemonade fountain and, oh – I cannot say it!"

"Say what? Say it!" commanded Lewis.

"He is *eating* the Statue of the Creators!" Slashermite wrung his hands in agitation and distress, his finger-blades catching and scraping metallically.

"He's *eating* it?!" gasped Jack. "The greedy little toe-rag!"

"Well . . . we *did* make it out of chocolate," pointed out Lewis. He and Jack had worked together on all kinds of landscaping and decoration and sculptures for Tauronia's town square over many weeks. The statue of them both was just for fun, but even though it was made of rich milk chocolate on a large chocolate-fudge plinth, no Taur or Mite would ever try to eat it. Electrotaur and Slashermite had made it plain to the inhabitants of Tauronia that the Creators would be pretty cheesed off if they ever lost a toe or an elbow.

"Slashermite – just tell Electrotaur to get him and bring him back!" said Aunt Thea.

"B-but, Lady Thea, he cannot! He is so angry that his power dial has shot up to maximum! He is dangerous to touch! He is afraid of electrocuting your cousin – and he's so fearfully cross he can't reset his dial!"

Jack sighed. The power dial on Electrotaur's chest was meant to make life easier, but when his Taur got very agitated it seemed to have a mind of its own. The only way to sort it out was to push the reset button – and only Jack had ever attempted to do that. It was dangerous. Very dangerous.

"Can't you just draw—?" began Aunt Thea but Jack stood up.

"No! No, I'm going in. There's nothing else for it. We could draw and draw and never know if it would work with Timmy. He's a human in Tauronia – he's messing up all the rules and the balance! If we don't get him out of there now anything could happen – anything! Sitting here drawing is no good."

"Jack, I forbid it!" cried his aunt, but her voice was wobbly and he knew she was beginning to see his point.

"If you're going, I'm going too!" said Lewis. "You're not leaving me behind."

"Right – we'll both go," said Jack. "Aunt Thea,

please, draw up Invisitaur and get him to meet us at the bottom of the steps. He can hide us if we need him to."

"I'll go in – I can't let you two go," insisted their aunt.

"But you don't know the terrain like we do!" argued Jack. "You don't know which of the Taurs are goodies or baddies or what they can do or how you can defeat them."

Aunt Thea looked horrified, but she took the crayons and the mead and the paper. She knew Jack was right. "If you two don't come back. . ." she began.

"We will! And we'll bring Timmy too. Please – just draw!"

Aunt Thea began to draw as Jack and Lewis stepped towards the door to Tauronia, their hearts thumping with wild excitement. "Remember, he won't last," warned Aunt Thea. "None of my drawings ever do. They go shaky and wobbly after a while and then they fade away or just fall apart. It's really most disappointing."

"There's nothing wrong with your drawings," said Lewis sadly. "It's just that you don't believe in them enough. I know you're a grown-up, but you've got to try harder." He turned and followed

Jack into the standing stone. The golden light shone around his feet as he went down the stone steps, spiralling around until he could no longer see any moonlight from the world above.

"Tauronia," he murmured, holding on to Jack's shoulder, a little further down. "At last! Here we come."

Chapter Twelve

Choc and Shock

Before they got their first sight of the world they had created, Jack and Lewis got their first smell. It was glorious. Rich, exciting and thrilling – the smell of freshly cut grass (Lewis's favourite smell) mixed with the eggy whiff of sulphur from the volcano and the lava swamps, the ever present scent of spun sugar on a steady breeze down the valley from the Candyfloss Fields of Doom, the salty tang of the Tauronian Sea, the chocolate waft from the statue in the town centre . . . or what was left of it if Timmy really had begun eating it . . . the pungent odour of truck tyres. Jack tried to remember where that came from, but he forgot all about it as they finally reached the bottom of the spiralling stone steps.

A golden light bathed them fully now and a scene of colour and brilliance was laid out before them. The centre of Tauronia was a huge valley, a bit like something out of *Jurassic Park*, thought Jack. He knew Lewis must have been thinking of that when they had first thought up Tauronia a couple of years ago. It was surrounded by mountains and had a river running along the bottom of it, with many waterfalls tumbling down the mountains into it along the way. The river ran down to the Tauronian Sea, which was a sparkling aquamarine vision. Jack could see Spoonfish leaping up out of it in graceful arcs. They were like swordfish, only with spoons. They could spoon you to death if you annoyed them, but mostly they just spooned up the sherbert sand on the sea bed and ate it whenever they got hungry.

The valley was filled with woods and meadows

and fields of odd crops, like the candyfloss bushes, and there was the orchard of jam-tart trees. High in the mountains were several impressive castles with tall turrets and billowing flags. The best of these, made of gold with jewel-encrusted pointy bits, belonged to Electrotaur and Slashermite. To the north lay a large, ominously rumbling volcano, with molten lava endlessly trickling down its sides, pooling into a red-gold swamp at the bottom. The swamp was surrounded by glistening black rocks, which contained it and protected the rest of the valley. Draped over one of these rocks they could see Lavataur, lazily cooling his edges until they went grey and crispy. He waved a pumice-stone claw at them and they waved back, grinning with amazement.

Overhead, assorted Dragotaurs flapped magnificently, and flocks of small Aviamites flitted with impressive speed, glittering like winged jewels, trying to avoid getting eaten.

Below Electrotaur and Slashermite's castle lay a small town of higgledy-piggledy houses. Jack and Lewis didn't have much time for buildings which weren't castles or haunted mansions, so the houses and shops and other buildings around the town square were a bit badly drawn. Their windows were all kinds of odd shapes, their chimneys looked positively dangerous and many of the houses leaned sideways at an alarming angle. Still, the inhabitants of Tauronia seemed happy enough with them. Taurs and Mites of all kinds were looking out of the doors and windows, fascinated and shocked by what was happening in the town square.

The town square itself was almost empty. From where they stood, up on a little knoll where the stairway to the Overworld (as all Taurs and Mites called it) opened out, they could see Timmy, a small figure, standing on the edge of the large fudge plinth. Lewis squinted at the distant figure and then huffed out angrily, "He's eating my ear!"

"That's the least of our worries," said Jack. And he was right. Standing a few metres away from

Timmy was Electrotaur, and they could see from here that he was buzzing furiously, vibrating the paving slabs beneath his feet and sending showers of furious sparks in all directions from the tips of his claws and tail and the burning green fury of his eyes. His lame red-and-yellow checked trousers were steaming and Jack feared they might be about to burst into flames.

As far as Jack could tell, Timmy was so lost in scoffing Lewis's ear that he hadn't even noticed the angry Taur behind him.

Jack made to grab Lewis's arm and start running but just then Lewis looked up and pointed. There was a strange sound – a bit like a plastic kite in a gust of wind. Jack looked up too and blinked. Standing over them was an odd creature which looked as if it had been made of see-through cellophane – the kind that you wrap posh Easter Eggs with – and wire coat hangers. It was a bit like a pterodactyl in shape, as far as he could make out. Set into its narrow, pointy, transparent face were large round eyes which looked exactly like large marbles, even with the little blade of colour – blue, in this case – running through them, and its teeth looked like tiny icicles. It faded in and out of view in a rather insubstantial way.

"Invisitaur!" cried Lewis. "It's the Taur that Aunt Thea made! She's drawn it here for us, just like she promised. "Come on, Vizzi! Wrap us up and make us invisible!"

Invisitaur nodded its pointy peak thing and lifted its huge wings – at least four metres across the full span, thought Jack – before wrapping them down over the boys and Slashermite with a soft rustle. They could see very well through the covering, although it rippled a little, as if they were looking through fine silk, and as they began to move hurriedly down the hill towards the Tauronian town square, Invisitaur drifted along with them quite happily, without any stumbling or treading on their heels. He smelled faintly of almonds, thought Lewis. It didn't surprise him. Aunt Thea loved marzipan.

As they reached the town square Timmy was still obliviously stuffing his face despite the angry buzzing and sparking noises and the occasional harsh shout from Electrotaur. As they moved closer, still invisible beneath Invisitaur's wings, it became clear *why* Timmy wasn't paying attention to Electrotaur. His ears were still full of Stinkermite's pink goo – setting hard like rubber by the look of it. A good deal of it was still over his

head too, like a tight-fitting pink hood. Timmy looked like one big, unattractive pixie.

"Oi!" Lewis shot out from under Invisitaur's wing and poked Timmy in the shoulder. "Stop eating my ear!" He noticed that both his and Jack's noses were bitten clean off, too. And Jack's left elbow.

Timmy stopped and looked around at him. His initial flicker of fright was quickly replaced by his usual gloating face. "I've ett your nose. I've ett your nose!" he sang, poking his tongue out to reveal some part of one of his cousins melting on it.

"You idiot!" said Jack, also springing out into view. "Here you are in the middle of the most dangerous place imaginable and all you can do is stuff your stupid face with chocolate!"

"Not just *any* chocolate," grinned Timmy. "It's *your* chocolate! That's why I had to eat it. You both think you're so important! You've even made yourselves into a statue! Well, *I* think you're just a couple of dur-brains and you deserve to get eaten!"

"YOU WILL STOP!" bellowed Electrotaur, behind them, and now their hair began to stand on end, so great was the furious electrical charge that was radiating out from him, and the ground beneath them was beginning to shake and steam. Jack looked at his Taur and felt pride. Electrotaur was bristling with anger and desperate to defend his creator's chocolate likeness, but he had remembered what Jack had told him – that if he ever touched a human being while he was on the top notch of his power dial, he would electrocute them. And that was utterly, utterly forbidden.

"Well done, Leccy!" he said. "Can you just – um – let me. . .?" He reached out to the button on the centre of Electrotaur's chest, and his Taur opened his arms out to allow his creator to jab at it. In an instant, Electrotaur clicked off. His eyes shrank down to two tiny green dots, like a TV on standby, and there was a moment of silence. Jack blew out a relieved sigh and then pressed the button again. A second later there was another click and then a gentle humming picked up again and Electrotaur switched back on. He continue to stare balefully at Timmy, but managed to restrain his fury to just the occasional angry shower of sparks.

But Timmy had turned around and seen Electrotaur by now – and his face was white with shock, framed in its pink plastic snood.

"Come on – we've got to get you out of here," said Jack. "Get under Invisitaur's wings and we'll go now."

But incredibly, Timmy was folding his arms and pursing his white, scared lips into a shaky pout. "You're not the boss of *me*!" he sulked. "I'm not going anywhere until I get my own mead!"

All around them, Taurs in the shops and houses murmured and one or two windows were opened wider. If Timmy looked around him properly he would freak. But he was staring mutinously at Jack and still refusing to move, Lewis's chocolate earlobe now slowly melting in his hand.

Jack sighed and then looked over Timmy's shoulder. He took a deep, slow breath, reminding himself to count slowly to five and not panic. Lewis gripped his arm, his eyes like saucers. He had just seen what Jack had seen. "Taur trouble," he whimpered. He did not mean all the weird and wonderful creatures which were hanging out of their wonky doors and windows, watching the action by the statue. Oh no. They were no trouble. Nothing at all compared to what Jack and Lewis were looking at.

Over Timmy's shoulder they had a good view of one of the many winding roads that led down into Tauronia's town square. Moving rapidly along it were two other Taurs. Big Taurs. Big, *bad* Taurs. Jack gulped and Lewis gave a small moan of panic. Rumbling slowly but resolutely towards them on vast caterpillar-tyre tracks, were Grippakillataur and Krushataur. Jack remembered now – this was where the truck tyre smell came from, which he'd noticed as they'd stepped into the valley.

Krushataur was built like a warped kind of digger and had a boxy metal body with yellow and black hazard stripes down the sides. He was quite

crab-like, with two swirly red antenna-like eyes on steel rods and huge block-like pincers. He could crush boulders just for fun, and often did. He liked to eat them in pieces – he had a high-fibre diet – chucking them into his digger-like mouth. But occasionally, when he got mad, he also liked to pop the heads of creatures which got in his way, like Jack or Lewis could squish a grape between finger and thumb.

Grippakillataur – his big brother – was worse. Twice the size and a hulking beast made of rusty red iron girders, his eyes were eight tiny black dots in the centre of his metal head, like a spider's; his large round nostrils, high on the corners of his head, constantly snorted out exhaust and his mouth was basically a huge car crusher. He liked to snatch up his unhappy victims with his grippa

claws and then chuck them into his huge metal gob before ratcheting up his lower jaw and pulping them flat on his nasty green tongue and drinking the goo. He'd then spit out the dried-up remains.

Jack had made Krushataur and Lewis had made Grippakillataur. How they had laughed at the time. Oh ha. Oh ha ha ha.

"Quick!" squeaked Jack. "Under Invisitaur, now!" He grabbed Timmy and hauled him away from the chocolate statue. Timmy started to complain again, but as he was spun around he glanced across the town square and saw what his cousins had seen.

"Mummy!" he whimpered, as Jack yanked him under the rustly protection of Aunt Thea's Taur alongside Lewis.

Electrotaur stood still outside and glared at the oncoming beasts as they entered the square,

rumbling and shrieking as their metallic hulks got excited. He looked ready to square up to them, thought Jack. And that was so *not* a good idea, even for Electrotaur, who was eight foot tall and could be very mean. "Psst! Electrotaur! Don't! Just run away!" urged Jack, as they all edged backwards under the filmy cloak of Invisitaur.

"MUST STAY," replied Electrotaur. "MUST PROTECT CREATORS."

"It's OK," whispered Lewis as they reached the edge of the town square and the start of the road that led back up to the exit to Overworld. "They can't see us!"

Electrotaur turned and gave Lewis a pitying look. "The Lady Thea makes bad drawing," he commented.

"Oh – everyone's a critic," said Lewis, remembering how Slashermite had complained about his rubbish tail the very first time they had met. Then he realized what Electrotaur meant. While they had been creeping away, watching the action through the filmy wings of Invisitaur, they hadn't noticed the filmy wings getting a lot less filmy. They were so un-filmy now, that they weren't actually filmy at all. In fact . . . they weren't *there* at all. Only Invisitaur's spiky see-through teeth and blue marble eyes still remained, hovering somewhere above them, looking rather wretched.

"Oh no," wailed Jack. "She said it might not last! And she was right."

Lewis winced. "She just didn't believe it enough! She's too grown-up."

Grippakillataur swung his car-crusher chin around to face them, his caterpillar-tyre tracks leaving rubber skid marks across the flagstones. His huge green tongue slurped around his rusty teeth and he made lip-smacking noises. Krushataur chortled and then made a whistly hooting noise like an old steam train, before spinning around too and picking up speed towards them.

"What are we going to do?" squeaked Lewis. "They're baddies. They're totally baddies and I can't remember what defeats them."

Electrotaur ventured a suggestion. "RUN!"

And when even an eight foot electricity monster starts sprinting for its life, you know it's time to go.

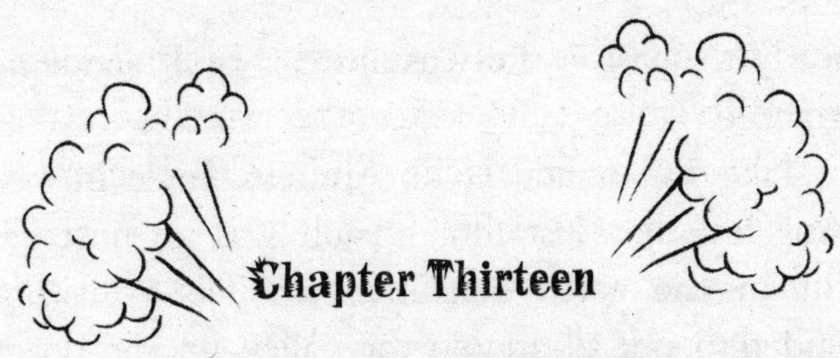

Chapter Thirteen

Unjust Dessert

How hilarious it had seemed to Jack and Lewis, so many months ago, when they had made Tauronia such a mad, whacky, dangerous, entertainingly unpredictable land. Back then, lying on their backs on the grass by the standing stone, the sun shining and the birds twittering, pretending they were sinking down through the earth to their own magic land, it was all *hugely* amusing.

They had made up all sorts of clever things. Like the Custardreas Fault. At any time in Tauronia, the Custardreas Fault could crack. In any place. It was completely random and mad and whacky and oh so very funny. Right up until now.

As Jack, Lewis, Timmy, Slashermite and Electrotaur galloped up the winding road in panic, Grippakillataur and Krushataur surging along behind them, bellowing and whistling and getting

ready to feast – the Custardreas Fault suddenly cracked.

Like the famous San Andreas Fault in Los Angeles, the Custardreas Fault was an unstable rift in the earth beneath their feet – it ran underground, all around the valley, up and down the mountains and the volcano and even under the sea, leading to sudden earthquakes. Boffinotaurs in Clever Castle (a small grey one at the far end of the valley with giant neatly sharpened pencils for turrets) liked to study its habits and predict the next time and place when a quake would occur. Because when the fault went – it went totally custard.

"Hurry! Get going! We're starting to lose them!" yelled Jack, and indeed, the baddie Taurs on their heels *were* actually struggling a bit as they pushed hard uphill. The lower jaw of Grippakillataur's huge car-crusher mouth was very heavy and given to dragging down on to the ground from time to time, sending up a shower of red sparks and making a dreadful scraping noise. And when that happened, Krushataur, madly swinging his boulder-crushing pincers around behind, would cannon into the back of him with bellows of annoyance.

But just as they were only twenty seconds from

the exit to Overworld there was a terrifying judder through the ground and out of nowhere a huge chasm cracked open just beneath Slashermite's feet.

Lewis screamed, "Slashy! Slashy! Jump!"

Poor Slashermite hurled himself forward as the chasm widened beneath him and thrust his finger-blades out hard. He crashed into the ragged edge of the torn earth and his blades drove deep into it, anchoring him high above a newborn cliff which plunged down to terrifying depths. As the chasm widened, he was suddenly five metres away from them, scrambling back up to the top.

He turned around and stared back at them as they all clustered along the edge of the chasm. Lewis stared down and gulped. Far, far below them it was yellow. Very yellow. And rising.

And catching up fast behind them, steaming and creaking and clunking and whistling and lip-smacking with excitement, were Krushataur and Grippakillataur.

"What's it to be?" murmured Lewis. "Death by crushing or death by custard?"

He knew that at any second a huge eruption of molten custard would spew up out of the chasm. He knew it because he had drawn it.

"Slashermite! Quick! Run up to Aunt Thea! Tell her she's got to draw us another exit!" bellowed Jack.

"Quick! Do as he says!" agreed Lewis, as Slashermite looked uncertainly across the chasm. "Where, though, Jack? We have to know!" he added urgently.

"Tell her," bellowed Jack, grabbing Timmy just before he fell into the chasm, so mesmerized was he by the churning yellow gloop below, "to put the exit in the base of the chocolate statue. In the fudge plinth! Hurry!"

"Do that!" shouted Lewis and now they were hurtling along again, skirting the curved line of the Custardreas Fault as pleasant vanilla-scented steam began to rise from it.

"Smells nice," murmured Timmy, bumping along in a daze.

"*So* not good!" wailed Jack. He had seen Lewis's drawings and he knew what followed that nice smell.

Krushataur and Grippakillataur were hot on their heels again now, rumbling along the edge of the chasm, oblivious to the danger. Krushataur was still waving his massive blocky pincers around like a disco dancer and whistling with glee as he bore down on them.

Electrotaur abruptly swung down and picked up Timmy, who was lolloping along grizzling loudly and slowing them down. Timmy squealed as he was tucked under the big Taur's arm, but Jack and Lewis just ran faster, back down the hill towards the square again. There was another rumble beneath their feet and then a glugging noise, like the world's biggest pudding coming to the boil.

Jack grabbed Lewis's and Electrotaur's arms and bellowed, "DOWN HERE! NOW!" He had spotted one of their many cave openings in the steep hill they were plunging down, and now he dragged them all into it, Timmy flopping along in Electrotaur's armpit, just in the nick of time.

As they hurled themselves deep into the little cave, which had nice soft green moss on its floor and small glowing stalactites hanging from its low

ceiling, the custard blew. Jack poked his head out once and saw a huge yellow steaming geyser shoot up from the chasm further up the hill. It was joined by six or seven other custard geysers all the way along the fault. Jack ducked back inside just as a custard avalanche billowed down the hill. They saw it shoot past the mouth of the cave – a cloud of sweet-smelling, boiling doom . . . it went on for several seconds and then, abruptly, stopped.

Everything went very quiet. You couldn't help thinking of treacle tart, thought Lewis.

Then Jack poked his head out again. Back up the slope all was yellow. Including two huge dripping statues of very bad Taurs. Jack pulled the others out of the cave. "Come on . . . we can't stay here. We've got to keep moving. Aunt Thea will be frantic."

They picked their way down, slipping and sliding in the custard, which had quickly cooled to a pleasant bath-water temperature. Just as Jack began to breathe out he heard a clank. And a very sticky whistle. He looked back just in time to see Krushataur tumble backwards into the chasm. Phew! But – oh no – Grippakillataur was also sliding . . . down towards them. His jaw was crashing up and down in fury, sending spurts of

custard out in all directions, and his caterpillar tracks weren't holding, so he was skidding down towards them, faster and faster.

"Go! Go! Go!" shrieked Jack, pushing everyone forward. They stumbled back into the town square, running at the statue from a different angle now. The custard avalanche had petered out quickly up on the hill and not reached the square, so their feet – thankfully – didn't slide any more. They tore towards the fudge plinth and saw, to their immense relief, a tall door opening in it, revealing stone steps. Then Timmy fell over and Lewis fell on top of him and Electrotaur fell on top of them both.

"Get up! Get UP!" screamed Jack. Lewis looked up and saw something awful reflected in his brother's huge, scared eyes. Grippakillataur bearing down on them all.

Lewis had drawn Grippakillataur, so Lewis knew the terrible truth.

There was absolutely no escape.

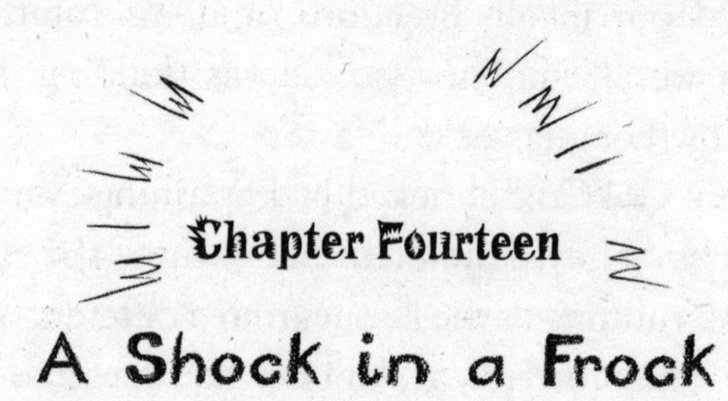

Chapter Fourteen

A Shock in a Frock

Electrotaur roared and Timmy squealed. Jack stared back in horror as Grippakillataur's huge car-crusher jaws snapped shut. There was a horrible crunching noise. Lewis was yelping with fright and Jack felt his head start to spin with the shock of it all. This was Tauronia. REAL Tauronia, and Grippakillataur really *had* got Electrotaur by one of his arms. Electrotaur was shaking and sparking and roaring with fury as his poor arm was pulped between Grippakillataur's jaws.

Meanwhile Timmy had been pinched up into the air in one of the Taur's huge claws. He was swinging by the seat of his trousers and emitting a non-stop guffathon of terror.

Jack and Lewis were frozen to the spot. They wanted to run, but they had to rescue Electrotaur and Timmy and they just did not know how. Then

there was a sudden cool rush of air behind them and a polite voice said, "I say, stand aside, will you? Got a bit of a job to do."

They spun round and saw a man on a shining white horse, clad in a scarlet jacket with gold braiding and buttons, his legs in riding trousers and shiny brown boots and his wavy blond hair flying out behind him as he pulled his whinnying horse up on to its back legs. "Unhand that boy and that Taur!" bellowed the man in a commanding voice. He pulled a shining silver sword out of his belt and drove it directly up Grippakillataur's right nostril. The giant Taur shrieked so loudly Jack thought his ears might burst, but it unclenched its huge jaws to do so and Electrotaur immediately scrambled out backwards. He stood up, and lifting his remaining arm, shot a jet of blue electricity from his fingertips directly up Grippakillataur's other nostril. "I ANGER!" he bellowed. "I ANGER MUCH!"

Grippakillataur hiccupped and then began to shake violently as Electrotaur continued to blast a crippling jet of electricity into him. Timmy still dangled, high above their heads in Grippakillataur's dangerously trembling claw.

"Stop!" yelled Jack, as the strange man went to

attack the Taur's other nostril again. "If he lets go, Timmy will fall and break his neck!"

The stranger held back, looking worried, and Timmy continued to dangle. The only thing dropping was gas. Lots of it. And this was to save Timmy's life. A zzzzzubbing sound cut through the metallic rumbling noise from Grippakillataur and Jack and Lewis looked wildly around, to see Stinkermite zooming across the town square towards them.

He was still in his Princess Flowerdew dress and now appeared to have some matching high-heeled fluffy sandals on, too. They didn't slow him down much. He clacked to their side in seconds, staring up hungrily at Timmy.

"Stinkermite!" yelled Lewis. "This is really not the time! Timmy is in dreadful danger."

"Guffy, guffy! Top-quality panic variety!" marvelled Stinkermite. "Thirty per cent hydrogenated vegetable fat, forty-one per cent cocoa, forty per cent sugar, three per cent bogie. No other guff smells like it or lasts like it!" Now he was puckering up his lips.

"I say! This is somewhat improper," observed the man on the horse. "I think you should at least introduce yourself first!"

Stinkermite paid no attention. The dribbly goo was once again spewing up into the air and spinning around. As Electrotaur continued to hold Grippakillataur in an electrical spasm, Jack and Lewis stared, appalled and mesmerized, at Stinkermite's pink bubble. Above them, Timmy was gargling and squeaking and staring in horror at the bubble as it came for him a second time.

But instead of engulfing Timmy once more, this time the bubble stayed beneath him, getting bigger and wider, and at last it was complete, because Stinkermite sealed it off with his slippery green lips and then stepped back. His proboscis did not shoot out. He just looked around at everyone, with a rather proud expression.

"It's a soft landing! He's made a soft landing!" gasped Lewis, and Stinkermite nodded and fiddled with his lacy sleeves, self-consciously.

"Huzzah!" shouted the strange man on the horse and thrust his sword up Grippakillataur's right nostril for the second time, just as Electrotaur whacked in a few more volts of electricity. The giant baddie Taur spasmed and as he did so, he let go of Timmy, who plopped down instantly on to the pink bubble mattress below him. As Grippakillataur tipped backwards

on his caterpillar tracks and conked out altogether, Timmy lay on the pink bubble for a few seconds, like a dazed starfish, and then began to sink, slowly, into it.

"Oh, guffy! Guffy!" gurgled Stinkermite joyfully.

"Stinkermite!" said Jack. "Stop it!"

But Timmy was already sealed in, the proboscis was already out, and three seconds later their cousin was shrink-wrapped in pink goo all over again. And before either Jack or Lewis could stop him, Stinkermite had grabbed the pink Timmy-shaped blob and run off with him.

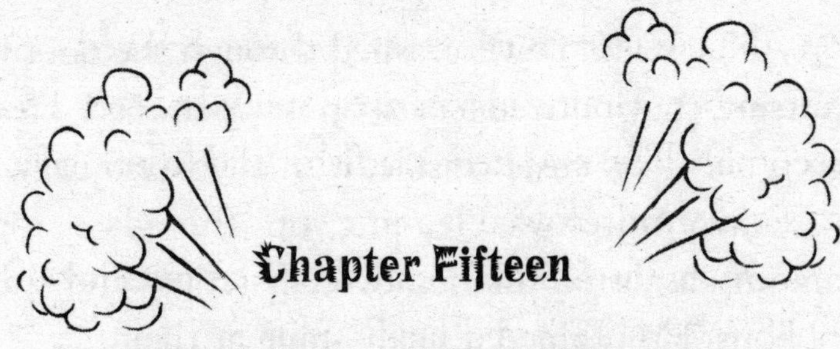

Chapter Fifteen

Stinkermite Style

Jack and Lewis immediately gave chase. Electrotaur made no attempt to run after them. His injured arm and his fight with Grippakillataur had left him almost completely out of energy. The stranger on the horse cantered after them, however. For a minute they couldn't see any trace of Timmy – but then they saw Stinkermite dragging him into one of the little wonky buildings around the Tauronian town square. They chased across to it and Jack gasped when he saw it was a shop with a sign above it reading:

STINKERMITE STYLE –
FROCKS & FRILLS FOR EVERY OCCASION.

In the window were assorted glamorous outfits which Princess Flowerdew would have stamped on her favourite elf for.

As Jack and Lewis crashed through the door in pursuit, they noticed a card on it which read: *Fresh guffs only – no credit*. Inside, it smelled very eggy.

Stinkermite was leaning on the glass top, among assorted diamanté hair clips and silk ribbons. He beamed a sickly smile at them.

"Stinkermite Style!" he dribbled (all over the glass). "How can I help?"

"What have you done with Timmy?" demanded Jack, as the stranger on the horse cantered about in the doorway.

"Timmy? Oh – *Timmy*! He lives with me now." Stinkermite smiled. "Timmy! Come show everyone! Come show!"

There was a muffled thud and then a door opened at the back of the little shop and Timmy stepped out. His jumper and pyjamas were gone and now he was resplendent in a purple sequinned ballgown. Little bits of pink goo still clung to his head and his little eyes were rather glassy. He opened his mouth to speak, but no words came out.

"You wish to buy? Thirty guffs. No – to you – twenty!"

"Stinkermite!" Lewis gave his creation a hard stare. "Timmy does not live with you and he doesn't belong in Tauronia. Hand him over."

"Wait though," said Jack. "Perhaps Timmy *does* belong in Tauronia." Lewis stared at his big brother.

Timmy began to whimper. "No! No! Take me home. I'll be good, I promise. . ."

"I don't know. I think it's too much of a risk. Nobody will know what happened to you and everything will be OK for *us*. . ." weighed up Jack, remembering Timmy's nasty rhymes and threats about Aunt Thea. "Your mum and dad will get over it. And at least we'll never have to worry about Aunt Thea getting arrested."

"No – no I promise! I won't say anything about it to anyone – not ever!" wept Timmy. "I don't want to live with a guff-eating mo-o-onster . . . I don't want to wear princesses' dre-e-e-esses. . ."

Jack put his head on one side. "Seems a shame for Stinkermite. He's really taken to you!"

"No-o-o," begged Timmy. "Don't leave me."

"Ahem," said the horse-riding stranger, politely, from the door. "I think you might wish to speed up your negotiations." Through a curtain of feather boas and pink tights, Jack could see through the shop window to the square. Electrotaur was waving at them, desperately, with his remaining arm, and beside him, Grippakillataur's caterpillar tracks were quivering – he was waking up.

"Come on!" Jack leaped over the counter and grabbed Timmy, ignoring Stinkermite's squawk of disappointment. He dragged his cousin out of the shop where the stranger grabbed him and hauled him up, with a swish of fabulously sparkly frock, on to the saddle behind him. They tore back to the opening in the statue plinth and Jack and Lewis piled into it just as Grippakillataur began to launch himself upright again. Electrotaur hurtled wonkily in behind them, his pulped arm dangling and sparks bouncing off the walls, and then the man on the horse, carrying Timmy, ducked down into the stone staircase too.

"Make haste!" cried the stranger as his horse snorted and clip-clopped on the steps behind them, Timmy clinging on at the back. "This is an unreliable exit. It may crumble at any time. There is not a moment to lose!"

And he was right. Even as they scrambled up the dimly lit stairwell Jack could see the stone steps flickering and fading. He shoved Lewis harder. "Get a move on! It's breaking up! It's not going to last!"

There was a crumbling noise and then a terrible ramming thud, and Jack looked back again to see Grippkillataur bashing his car-crusher jaw up the insubstantial stairwell behind them. Lewis bashed

open a door and they all stumbled out into the fresh air of the Overworld. The still, calm sky spread over them, the moon low in the west and the stars shining prettily down.

Jack and Electrotaur followed – and then the man on the horse, carrying Timmy, emerged into the cool night breeze of the Overworld.

"I want my mum," whimpered Timmy. Then he fainted again.

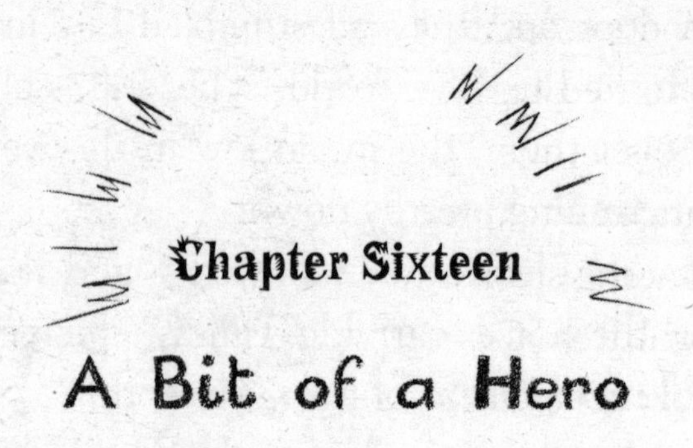

Chapter Sixteen

A Bit of a Hero

Jack looked around, confused. The garden looked wrong . . . then he realized that they hadn't come back out of the standing stone. They had emerged from a different doorway which blinked and shook insubstantially in the middle of Aunt Thea's favourite rose bush. Aunt Thea and Slashermite were nowhere to be seen.

They could still hear Grippakillataur bellowing far below them. Jack pushed the door quickly shut, and it sort of frayed at the edges and then blinked away with a rustle of rose-bush leaves.

"This boy should live, but he needs a physician," said the stranger, getting down off the horse and laying Timmy on the grass.

Jack winced as he looked at Electrotaur – the mangled, splattered flat remains of his arm, hanging from his shoulder like a piece of modern art.

"Where's Aunt Thea?" asked Lewis. "And Slashermite?" He glanced back at the standing stone. The light from Tauronia could still be seen glowing from behind it. "You don't think. . ." he gulped. "I mean . . . she wouldn't have. . ."

"The Lady Thea has gone into Tauronia?! We must rescue her! At once!" proclaimed the horse-riding man. "Without 'ere a backward glance! There is no time to be lost!" He pulled on the reigns and his white horse reared up, ready to charge up the garden. The horse was looking a bit see-through.

"But she wouldn't!" said Lewis. "Would she. . .?"

"She was probably thinking we were *never* coming out through *her* door," said Jack. He bit his lip. "She must have got desperate and decided to see if we'd climbed across the custard chasm after all."

"Then I must away to save her!" declared the horse-rider.

Jack looked up at the man and felt he knew him somehow. "Have we met before?" he asked.

"Partly," replied the man. "Make haste! The Lady Thea is in danger – and this boy needs a physician. He is decaying!"

"No, he always smells like that," assured Lewis, prodding Timmy with his toe. Timmy snuffled but didn't wake up.

"Jack! Lewis!" They spun around and saw Aunt Thea running towards them – not from the back of the standing stone but up the garden. "You're safe! Oh, thank goodness!" She was clutching paper and crayons, and Slashermite, bouncing along behind her, held a twiggy bottle of Merrion's Mead.

"We ran out of mead and had to get more from the kitchen," explained Aunt Thea. "We thought the exit wasn't working and that more mead might do it! We thought you were *never* going to come out! Oh, Jack! Lewis! Are you all right?" she gasped as she reached them. "Are you hurt?"

"No, we're OK," said Jack. "But Timmy's unconscious."

"Well, that's a blessing, anyway," said Aunt Thea.

"But Electrotaur's *really* hurt," added Jack.

Aunt Thea grimaced when she saw poor

Electrotaur's arm. "Oh, Electrotaur! How dreadful. It must be agony!"

"I TWINGE," admitted Electrotaur.

"Quick," said Jack. "Hand over the paper and the crayons. Slashermite – do you think you could help Electrotaur back down into Tauronia?"

"What? Are you nuts?" said Lewis. "He's only just escaped!"

"I know. But if we get him to retrace his steps back down into Tauronia where all the damage happened, we can draw his arm all right again and he should be OK."

"Why not just do it up here?" asked Aunt Thea. "It's too dangerous down there."

"No," insisted Jack. "Lewis can draw Grippakillataur back in his cave now, and Krushataur's already fallen into a custard-filled chasm. There won't be another custard eruption for a good few hours, because there's only one a day, at most. And what's been done in Tauronia needs to be undone in Tauronia or we can't be sure it'll stay undone. Slashermite can look after him on the way down, in case he faints or something."

"Allow me!" cried the horse-riding man, who was actually *not* riding a horse any more. "Do not risk your small Taur! I would be

honoured to go back in with this mighty warrior."

Jack was impressed. "You're a hero, aren't you?"

The man nodded and beamed at him, shaking a stray lock of glorious golden hair back off his fine high forehead.

"But," went on Jack regretfully, "you can't help." He waited while the man bumped down on to the grass. "Your legs have gone."

"Always the legs," sighed the hero, tilting sideways slightly.

"I'm sorry," said Aunt Thea. "I really am."

"You drew him, didn't you, Aunty?" asked Jack.

She nodded and looked embarrassed. "Yes. You see, Jack, I've travelled the world in hopes of meeting a hero – a real, decent, proper hero. And I've never found one yet. So when I came back off my holiday I had a bit of a wild moment and decided to see if I could draw one. And so I did – then I spilled the mead on the drawing and hey presto – I got my hero! Isn't he glorious? Apart from having no legs, of course."

"And half a head," added Lewis. And it was true. The hero continued to semi-smile winningly at them all, but half his head had indeed now disappeared. Half a handsome Roman nose and one glorious blue eye still remained.

"Oh, it's so disappointing!" said Aunt Thea. "You find the *perfect* man and one minute he's declaring he'll be yours for ever and the next minute he's gone, leaving bits of himself strewn all over the house. Just like all the other men I've ever met, really. But it's not your fault." She patted him on his shoulder; the one shoulder now left which she *could* pat. "I just didn't believe in you enough."

Lewis shook his head sadly.

"So that's why I found that leg by the standing stone – and the arm and chest on the bench – and the hair. . ." said Jack.

"Oh dear, did you? How terribly, terribly embarrassing," said Aunt Thea.

"You just didn't believe in him enough to make him last," concluded Jack. "Just like Invisitaur."

"Don't blame yourself," said the hero, surprisingly clearly through his half a mouth. "I *am* too good to be true. . ." There was a thud as his half a head dropped down next to his remaining visible limb . . . the right leg this time. Jack noticed the horse had long since vanished. Aunt Thea stretched out a pointed toe in a bright red ankle boot, and nudged fondly at her hero's boot. It nudged fondly back and then fell over and vanished. The half-smiling half a head followed.

"Men," she sighed. "When the going gets tough, they fall to pieces."

"Oi," said Jack. "Men present!"

"Come on," said Aunt Thea briskly. "To work! Lewis – draw Grippakillataur back in his cave. Hurry! And, Jack – if Electrotaur is retracing his steps he'll have to go back down the route *I* drew . . . so you'd better re-draw the door in the rose bush *and* re-draw the passage I put in here, so it won't collapse this time."

Jack and Lewis set to work while Slashermite waited with Electrotaur by the rose bush. Jack traced over Aunt Thea's earlier drawing with his crayon and then tipped some mead on to it. The door

reappeared, looking steady and solid. Slashermite pulled its handle and it swung open smoothly,

sending a shaft of golden light across the garden.

"OK, the steps down should be stable now," said Jack. "Have you sorted out Grippakillataur, Lew?"

"Yep," said Lewis. "He's back in his cave, in bed."

Jack nodded at Electrotaur and his creation nodded back and stepped inside the rose-bush door once more. Slashermite hopped in anxiously after him and they both vanished from view. Lewis and Aunt Thea stood still, worrying and waiting.

"OK – I'll draw Electrotaur's arm back on now," said Jack, after a few seconds had passed. He grabbed some fresh paper and worked fast, recreating a glorious, scaly, strong arm and a hand with claws like lightning bolts. He tipped the mead on quickly and they waited, nervously, for the Taurs to re-emerge. Timmy had begun to snore, lying on the grass in his frock. It was a relief not to have to deal with him yet.

"Would . . . would you like me to draw your hero for you again?" offered Jack, when he'd finished Electrotaur's arm. "He should last for you then."

Aunt Thea smiled at him and shook her head. "No . . . it was a very silly idea. And lovely though he was, all that perfection could get a bit irritating."

The door in the rose bush suddenly flew open and out came Electrotaur, looking wonderfully

well, his arm swinging healthily from his shoulder. Slashermite bounced out behind him, grinning happily. "All is well! All is well!" he chortled and began to chase his own tail in mad circles around the lawn.

All of a sudden Timmy shot up on to his feet.

"Whaaaaaaaaaaaaaaaaaaa!" he commented. "THERE'S MONSTERS! MONSTERS!" He hurtled down the garden, screaming, and then tripped over his lacy skirt and fell face first into the compost heap.

Jack went to prod Electrotaur's arm and check it was OK. It was just as it should be, with the odd few sparks emitting from its fingertips. "Oh," Jack wailed, "why didn't I sort out his trousers while I was at it?" Electrotaur looked down at the red-and-yellow checked fashion disaster on his lower half and then, balefully, back at Jack. Jack took up his crayon.

"No, not now," said Aunt Thea, pulling Timmy up out of the compost heap. "Slashermite's got to hypnotize Timmy now – and then you've got to get him home and get that frock and all Stinkermite's goo off him before your parents wake up. Now, Lewis, get Slashermite to calm Timmy down and make him realize that all of this was a dream."

Slashermite could only hypnotize under Lewis's

instruction, so Lewis told him what to say and then they watched as his blades all shot out and began to waft backwards and forwards like a Mexican wave in front of Timmy's face.

"You are feeling very sleeeeepy," said Slashermite.

"Duh," said Timmy.

"You will go home with Jack and Lewis, clean off the goo and get back into bed and go to sleep."

"Duh."

"You will wake up in the morning feeling happy and knowing that everything that happened tonight was a dream."

"Duh."

Lewis whispered in Slashermite's ear.

"You will tell everyone who asks that Aunt Thea is wonderful in every way."

"Duh."

"You will eat more roughage."

Lewis whispered again.

"You will go to the bathroom to guff."

And just once more.

"You will ask for a Barbie for Christmas."

Jack and Lewis exploded with laughter and Aunt Thea sighed and pursed her lips, trying hard not to join in.

"Come on now – back down to Tauronia, you two," she said and gave Electrotaur and Slashermite each a goodnight kiss – on the cheek for Slashermite and on the chest for Electrotaur, as she couldn't reach his cheek.

"Come on, you three – get in the car and I'll drive you home," she said, as the Taurs stepped back into the rose-bush doorway to Tauronia and it vanished behind them with a gentle slurp. Further up the garden, the Standing Stone doorway also shut with a small zipping noise.

"No more mead, no more Taurs and no more heroes or wayward limbs," said Aunt Thea. "I really think that's all the madness I can deal with for a very long time!"

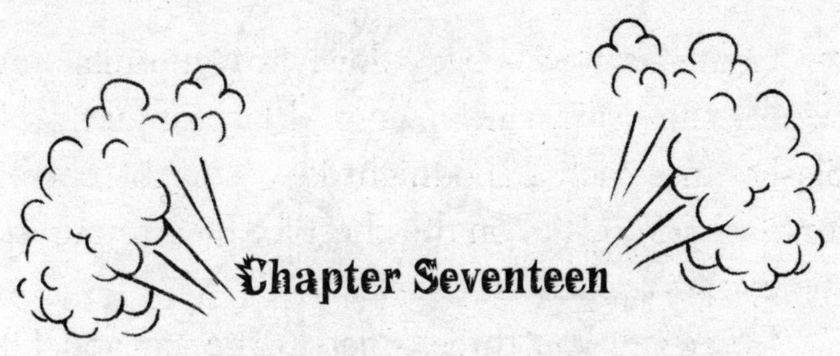

Chapter Seventeen

A Regular Guy

Aunty Di couldn't stand to be without Timmy a day longer. She and her husband had sorted out their "difficulties" and just after breakfast the next day she had come to collect him.

"Do you know, he's actually settled down quite well this morning," said Mum, with genuine surprise. She had been amazed when Timmy had arrived at the breakfast table and demanded All Bran. And chopped apple and banana. And orange juice.

Jack and Lewis said nothing.

There was no guffing. None at all. Probably, Jack thought, because Timmy had been so scared in the past twelve hours he was completely guffed out.

"Come on, poppet, time to go," said Aunty Di, pulling down the hood on Timmy's dressing gown to peck him on the cheek. "Ooh – what's that in your hair? Timmy . . . have you been eating bubble gum?"

"Um – yes, Aunty Di . . . we did have a bit of a bubble gum-blowing contest, didn't we, Timmy?" said Jack hurriedly. Getting all Stinkermite's pink goo off Timmy had proved impossible in the early hours of the morning. He and Lewis had tried to peel off as much as they could, but Timmy kept squeaking loudly every time they tried to get it out of his hair and they were afraid he'd wake Mum and Dad.

"Really, boys!" said Mum. "I had no idea you were doing that. You know I don't like you having bubble gum."

"We'll have to get some strong shampoo," murmured Aunty Di, trying to pick a lump off Timmy's hair. Timmy went to get his clothes and shoes on while his mum gathered all his stuff together in the hallway.

"Thank you so much, Cara," simpered Aunty Di, as they prepared to leave a few minutes later. "I'm sure

Timmy's had a *lovely* time, haven't you, darling?"

Timmy screwed up his face and tried to remember.

"Well, he got really wrapped up in things," chirped Lewis. Jack nudged him.

"They played all sorts of monster games, I expect," smiled their Mum. "Jack and Lewis love to pretend that their monsters are real! Honestly – sometimes I think they really believe it." Jack and Lewis grinned fixedly. "And they had tea with Aunt Thea."

Aunty Di looked less enchanted. "Oh – Thea," she said, with a thin smile.

Timmy turned around to face his mother. He fixed her solemnly with his little piggy eyes and said, "Aunt Thea is wonderful in every way."

His mother stared at him, then glanced uneasily around at them all. "Wonderful? Aunt Thea?"

"In every way," confirmed Timmy. "Oh – excuse me. I need to break wind. I must hurry to the bathroom." He ran into the under-stairs toilet and then re-emerged a few seconds later, smiling politely.

"Timmy, dear, are you quite all right?" Aunty Di was looking very anxious now.

"Do we have any prunes at home?" asked Timmy.

"Come on, sweetheart – time to go," gasped Aunty Di, grabbing her son's arm. "We can drop into the toyshop on the way home if you like . . .

buy you a treat for being such a good boy. And maybe some sweeties. . .?"

"Mixed nuts and seeds would be better for me," said Timmy.

"What *did* you two do to Timmy?" Mum asked, suspiciously, as they waved goodbye.

"Well," said Lewis. "We set a guff-chasing monster on him, which trapped him in a giant pink bubble and then sucked up all the guff gas, leaving him in a pink cocoon, then we accidentally sent him to Tauronia, where he was nearly drowned in custard and almost eaten by Krushataur and Grippakillataur because he'd been stuffing his fat face with *my* ear, but then he got saved by the guff-chasing monster and made to wear a princess dress, but in the end the man on a horse whose legs keep disappearing helped us rescue him."

Mum ruffled his hair and laughed. "Really, Lewis! The things you make up!"

"You can have a Gutwrencherzoid or a Blasterbitz Deathray if you want, poppet!" promised Aunty Di, sounding a little tense, as they walked down the path.

"Actually," said Timmy. "What I'd really like is a Barbie. . ."